D1177364

Leslie Anne MacDonald

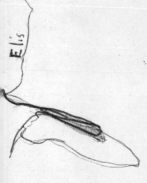

Elis

Prairie Colt

STEPHEN HOLT

Prairie Colt

Illustrated by
WESLEY DENNIS

GROSSET & DUNLAP

Publishers, New York

To my wife

MARGARET.

CONTENTS

ILLUSTRATIONS

Prairie Colt

Crazy Idea

EIF OLSON mounted the hot grandstand and slumped to a seat. Below him, on the backstretch of the track that ran by the stands, Jim Carroll's bay stallion, Combat Second, fought Whip McCarty's sorrel, Firebrand, for the lead of the Stockman's Race. The yearly race that always wound up the Lethbridge, Alberta, Fair.

Leif passed a hand across his eyes. Boy, it was hot! Hot and dry enough to make another no-good year for machinery sales. In fact, he and Big Chris, his dad, hadn't done any business the whole week of the Fair, and no business meant they'd soon be sunk.

Leif's machinery-scarred hand dropped from his eyes to softly riffle the pages of a full receipt book bulging the upper pocket of his blue shirt. Without wanting to he was looking off to the left, studying his dad's machinery exhibit. It stood, all neat and unsold, in its white-picketed yard.

"Bang!" Leif whispered, ruefully. "There goes dad's

agency to Bill Culp." Leaning back, Leif stared at a dry cottony cloud floating off toward the Rockies, and something within him squeezed shut. "I'm a poor salesman, and a bust, if I can't dope out some way to help dad."

Leif watched the two straining stallions rounding the turn for the finish line.

Roly-poly Soren Anderson, his dad's agency handyman, shouted, "Come on, Combat!"

A man behind Leif countered, "Yeah, Firebrand!"

Anna, on the other side of Leif, turned flushed cheeks to him, her rope-colored braids were shining round her pretty head.

"Oh, Leif," she breathed. "They're beautiful!"

The horses swept into the stretch, running low, straining every nerve for the lead.

Leif sat up, watching them: the bay, almost a red, big and rangy, plunging ahead, trying to fight off the speed of Firebrand, the sleek sorrel.

Something of the beauty of the battle stirred Leif, even with all his trouble. He gripped the raw edge of the pine seat and, with eyes on the big red horse, whispered, "Come on, Red. Red horse—run! What if I owned a red horse?"

But before Leif could see which swept across the finish line the victor, the man behind him jammed his hat down over his eyes.

Leif tore it off—and the race was over.

"Combat won." Soren, beside him chuckled.

Leif glanced to see if Soren had noticed his whisper. No, he guessed Soren hadn't. Leif breathed easier. Then he'd skip it—the crazy idea of owning a horse. Getting a colt and raising him up to win the Stockman's.

There was Big Chris, moving down the aisle and out to Jim Carroll. Big Chris, with the debts, who might lose the Interstate Harvester Agency, was the first to congratulate Carroll.

"Nice work, Jim." Big Chris' voice boomed up to Leif. "Must be great to own a running horse like that."

Leif jumped. There it was again—the idea of a red colt. It was so real he could almost see it. And the idea moved right into Leif's head, like a blue jay taking over a sparrow's nest.

Soren, getting to his feet, added wings to it. "Two thousand dollars, Leif." He chuckled. "That's what Carroll will get for Combat."

Leif nodded. It was true. The Stockman's was run for the privilege of selling the winner to breeders all over "The States" and Canada—Worth of Texas, Murphy of California—

"Two thousand dollars!" Anna Larsen's big blue eyes widened on Leif's. "That's a fortune."

Leif was having trouble with his breath. People getting out of the grandstand jostled him, but he scarcely noticed.

"Two thousand dollars," he whispered, his eyes following Big Chris' straight broad back and Jim Carroll's angular frame as they led Combat Second toward the stable—and the sale.

"If we had that!" Soren grinned. "I guess Mr. Culp'd whistle for the Agency. Even a promise of getting it and the Company would give Big Chris a break."

Leif was thinking hard, eyes on the father he worshipped. Big Chris wouldn't have to worry about that note with the Interstate Harvester if there was money like that in the offing. His blue eyes blazed with excitement. He had it to do. "If I could—if there was some way to get a colt. Raise him up to win the Stockman's. Put Big Chris in the clear—"

Soren turned to him.

Leif looked away in consternation. He must have said it out loud. For Soren was staring at him as though he'd lost his senses.

Anna, their housekeeper, her fingers strong from kneading bread, clutched his arm. "Leif, what a boy you are for having notions."

Leif couldn't offer much defense. But if it were something hard work could accomplish— He put his sun-browned hand up along his forehead.

"Sure, a touch of the sun," Soren said. He kept on saying it on the way home. When the Fair was only a memory Leif and Anna and Soren, packed into the front seat

of the Ford pickup truck, drove the thirty miles to
Magrath. This was the little prairie town where Big Chris
and Leif ran the Interstate Harvester Agency.

Leif, bent thoughtfully over the wheel, let Soren go on
kidding him. All he hoped was that Big Chris, who'd
stayed behind and would drive out later in his blue coupe,
might sell McCarty a new haying outfit.

They passed Carroll's ranch, and the boy looked at it
with new interest. There, over the paddock fence, Combat First, the sire of the horse which had won the Stockman's today, raced toward them.

Leif slowed down to watch the play of powerful rip-
pling muscles. How that stallion could run! He barely
heard Soren's scornful, "I suppose you'll buy one of
Combat's colts—five hundred dollars will fall out of a
cottonwood tree for that purpose, eh, Leif?"

Leif nodded, and as the graceful horse reached the
fence, then swerved and, with a high kick out behind,
fled up the paddock, he gave the truck more gas and
drove on toward home. This was too big to talk about
and, he had to admit it, he had too little to go on.

They reached Magrath, drove through the little white
painted town, clustered along the bank of a tree-lined
canal, and into the machinery-choked yard of the Interstate Harvester Agency.

Leif stopped the truck by the office building.

Anna got out, moving purposefully toward her gleaming kitchen.

"I'll have supper ready in half an hour—hot biscuits and fried ham, Leif," she said. "You be ready."

Leif nodded and drove the truck around the office and through the yard to the big machine shed. He sat staring at the two tractors, the dozen binders and ten plows as if he had never seen them before. He didn't know they were there.

"If I'm any good at all," he whispered, driving the truck inside the machine shed. "I'll get a colt. Raise him. And win that Stockman's for Dad."

He shut the motor off, got out of the truck and moved softly out into the machine yard. The slam of the door as he closed it settled it. He'd do it—

He moved around the side of the office wall and in through the front door.

Soren waddled in after him, to sit on the edge of the battered desk.

"You'd better stick to machinery, Leif," he advised, staring down at Leif's shock of blond hair, as the boy sat at the desk. "Colts are out of your line—you'll get skinned."

Leif brought his eyes up to Soren, then let them go past him to a brown letter file on a shelf back of the big iron stove.

"Notes Receivable—Outlawed," his lips read. Leif got up and brought the file over to the desk and, sitting down, began thumbing through the yellowed dog-eared worthless notes.

"Riley's for five hundred—no, not that one. It was hopeless. Culp's? That was okay, it shouldn't even be in this file. Ike Waite's? Leif's battered hands poised to throw it back into the file, then suddenly closed tighter on the note. Ike was a tough baby. A shiftless guy with a lot of broken-down work horses, and two or three old racing mares.

Soren, looking over Leif's shoulder, read his thoughts.

"I suppose you'll go up and collect from Waite," he scoffed. "A deadhead account. Then you'll go and buy a colt with the money—"

Leif just sat there, not shaking his head. He saw that racing colt so clearly in his mind. Ike was shiftless. He didn't look after his stock. No telling where his mares might have strayed—maybe one of them might bring a foal into the world out of Jim Carroll's Combat—

Leif, figuring on the chances, whistled softly and, standing up, gently folded the note and shoved it into his leather jumper pocket.

"Boy, oh boy!" he whispered. "If he could get hold of one of Ike's mares and bring her home. And she did happen to give him a foal out of Combat—"

Leif snapped the old file together and, putting it back on the shelf, made for the office door.

Soren tagged after him, protesting, "You're crazy. Plumb crazy. You're only sixteen. You'd better not get mixed up with that tricky Waite. Leave your Dad to take care of him."

Leif led Soren along the plank walk toward the little white house, and the smell of frying ham.

"I'll handle Waite," he told Soren, with more confidence than he felt. Ike Waite was sly. If he got the idea that Leif wanted one of his mares, well—he'd never let one go.

They entered the kitchen, washed at the kitchen stand, then sat down to hot biscuits and golden-brown fried ham.

Leif ate quickly and in silence, his mind on the office— and figuring out Ike Waite's note.

Soren sat opposite, his mouth full, and mumbling worriedly. He was fond of the boy.

Leif stuffed biscuits and ham down as fast as he could. In ten minutes he was back at the office desk, the note before him. The big kerosene lamp with the brass shade threw down a soft yellow light.

"Let's see," he said, figuring. "The note's for two hundred even, and it's five years old, with interest at six per cent—" Leif figured for some minutes, then leaned back to stare toward Pothole Coulee, where Waite lived in his tumble-down unpainted shack. "Two hundred and ninety-six dollars and ten cents," Leif whispered. "Allowing for the discount. That's what I'll offer to cancel off to Ike Waite for one of his mares—"

He ran fingers through his blond thatch, folded the note, together with his figures, and put the two papers back into his jumper pocket. Then he prepared to turn in. Anna gave him an encouraging smile over her knitting. Soren rattled his newspaper and said nothing.

"Boy—a live colt," Leif whispered, sitting down on the edge of the big white-iron bed he and Big Chris slept in. "A wonder horse—"

Suddenly, with a stuffy feeling under his chest, Leif dived under the big brown comforter. Reaching to the stand, he blew out the light, then lay staring out of the window that overlooked the yard. His eye caught the outline of the machine shed. And off to the right of it, the smaller outline of an old barn with a pole corral leading to it.

"A barn all ready," he breathed. "I'll fix up the place —buy a saddle." Lying there in the dark, Leif swallowed hard. "I'll get that mare from Waite," he breathed. "Got to." Suddenly, he turned on his side and slept.

It was late the next afternoon before Leif could get away to drive out to Waite's.

Culp, big and burly and envious of Big Chris owning

the agency, had brought in twine he hadn't used. Wanting a refund which he was entitled to, but putting Big Chris in deeper than ever.

Then followed an endless stream of farmers. Wanting to talk crop failure. Forcing Leif to listen politely.

But at length, with the last farmer cleared out, Leif paused only to brush his unruly hair into some kind of shape, then backed the pickup truck out of the shed.

Soren came out of the office to hoist his roly-poly body up beside Leif.

"Well," he said, earnest for once. "We ready?"

"We?" Leif stared.

"Sure, we." Soren's mouth made a tiny O. "Old Waite's too smart for you—just a kid."

Leif slowly shook his head. Soren'd be sure to let the cat out of the bag—let Ike know that what he wanted was an old mare for the note.

"Sorry, Soren," Leif said, firmly. "This is a one-man job."

Soren, shaking his head, rolled slowly out of the seat.

"Maybe that note's better than you think," he suggested. "Maybe Ike's got hold of some dough—and Chris could sure use it."

Leif paused. It was an idea. He shook his head at last. There wasn't a chance of Ike's getting any money. Everyone knew he'd been on the rocks for years.

"No, Soren," Leif said. "Anything I get out of Waite's note will be velvet, and you know it."

He started the truck and, with Soren's grumbling warning in his ears, drove north, then east to Pothole Coulee.

Ike Waite, lean and tall, with small rust-brown eyes under thin brows, was before the barn door, trying to back a bay mare inside, rump first. He left off fighting the mare's head as Leif drove up.

"Ornery?" Leif asked, shutting off his motor, and being very careful not to notice the mare—her lean legs, the deep heart-girth, and the intelligent breadth between her eyes.

"Naw!" Waite denied.

Leif cautiously got out of the truck and came over to stand by Ike. He knew the man was fibbing. The thing to do, Leif sensed, was to put lots of heat on Ike about his note. Pour it on hot, then wait for a break. If Ike offered the mare, turn him down cold.

Leif pulled the note from his pocket and, trying to make his face look like Big Chris' big broad one, said, "About this note you owe us, Mr. Waite. When are you going to pay it?"

Ike jumped as if stung. Leif thought afterward that he should have known Waite was putting on an act. Usually, he was just insolent.

"I won't pay it," he blustered. "I'm broke. And, any-way, the plow I bought with the money's worn-out. Beat it!"

Leif held his ground.

Softly, he said, "We've got to have a settlement. And now— It's been a dry year and we need money."

"Ye'll not git it," Waite howled.

Leif moved closer to Ike, his eyes steady, first on Ike, then on the mare. Boy, she was a beauty, and obviously going to foal. Leif's heart bounded. With the way Ike let his animals stray, there certainly was a chance the foal could be Combat's.

"Oh, yes, we will," Leif said slowly.

Ike bluffed.

Like two sparring roosters, they walked around each other. Then Ike put his big boot on the running board of the truck and tried pleading.

"Look at this farm," he bleated, waving toward the unpainted shack, the sagging windmill, the old barn. "Does this shebang look like I could pay a note for two hundred dollars?"

Leif stared off to the west at the sun going down be-hind Grizzly Pass. That Pass always gave him a funny feeling. It was as if it were going to mean something to him one day. Purposely, he avoided staring at the mare that he wanted more than anything else in the world right now.

"Two hundred and ninety-six dollars and ten cents," Leif corrected. "And I'm going to collect it. I've worked all day and—" he paused a moment, then slipped in the first hint. "Someway, I'm going to get payment." He swallowed, hoping Ike wouldn't notice, then added, "take something—"

Leif was conscious of Ike's voice toning down. A pair of sly eyes studied him.

"I see," Ike said. But the next minute he started raving again. "You can't get blood out of a turnip!" he shouted. Then, taking the mare's head, he started fighting her back to the barn door once more. "Git in there, Rebellious," he rasped, twisting the mare's head. "Rebellious, out of Impulse," he snorted to Leif. "Stubborn as they come—"

Leif took a deep breath and plunged in clean over his neck.

"Good thing you don't ask me to take her on the note," he said. Then suddenly opened the truck door and got inside and started the motor.

Ike paused.

Leif, fighting off a smothered feeling in his chest, leaned out of the cab and said, "Tomorrow we'll start suit on your note, Mr. Waite. I'm sorry, but we've got to have money." He let the truck in gear and with his heart in his mouth, drove clear to the gate leading to the highway. Wasn't Ike going to hail him?

Then Ike did. And came, leading Rebellious, to plop
a foot once more on Leif's running board.

" I ain't got a thing," he said, not meeting Leif's eyes.
A fact that within the half hour Leif was to sadly remember. "But, if you'll take this stubborn old mare—"

Would he? Leif staring at the slim mare, didn't trust
his voice. Just nodded. He brought out the note and
signed it, "Paid in Full." Wrote it across the face, then
handed it back to Ike, who burst into mocking laughter
as his fingers closed on it.

"That's good," he said, slapping a leg till the dust flew.
Leif puzzled.

A car pulled into the yard and stopped and Big Chris
got out and came across to them.

Ike Waite, still guffawing, waved the cancelled note in
front of Big Chris' eyes. But not before Big Chris had
told Leif why Ike was laughing. Not really telling him,
except by what he said to Waite: "I hear your uncle in
Vancouver died, Ike—left you some money. Maybe you'll
settle that note now. I need the money very much."

Leif, his eyes widening on the roll of bills Waite pulled
tauntingly from his worn overalls pocket, looked at Big
Chris.

For a full minute there was a dead silence.

Then Leif opened his mouth to explain. But Ike Waite
beat him to it.

"Leif's settled this note," Ike chortled, waving it in front of Big Chris' broad sunburned nose. "Settled for this old crow-bait mare."

Big Chris, in his blue-serge suit, and with gentle blue eyes still holding that smile, turned to Leif. And Leif had to explain.

Silence settled again over the three.

A dog from Blaha's farm, down the road, barked. A flock of mallard ducks wheeled over—bound for the grain field.

Suddenly, Big Chris took Leif's arm and looked deep into his eyes.

"That's great, Leif," he said, heartily. "You've got yourself a horse."

Ike's jaw dropped.

"Then, you aren't going to fight it?" he blurted.

Big Chris looked at Leif, then at Rebellious. His eyes crinkled. "I'll say I won't," he said softly. "Any deal Leif makes is okay with me."

Leif felt his insides go funny. What a dad to have. A fellow couldn't help wanting to help instead of letting Big Chris down this way.

"Rebellious," he whispered, watching his father walk toward his car. "You've got to have a colt out of Combat. You've just got to."

"Eh—what's that?" Ike demanded.

Leif waved to Big Chris pulling out of the yard for home, then moved for his truck. "Nothing, Mr. Waite," he said. "And I'll pick Rebellious up tomorrow."

He got into the cab, started the engine and drove slowly home to Magrath. There was the barn to fix up— things to do for Rebellious and her foal. The foal that just had to be a racing colt—

Fortunately, Big Chris had sold a machine after all, maybe two.

CHAPTER 2

Racer or Scrub?

THE NEXT MORNING, driving the pickup truck with the horse trailer on behind toward Ike Waite's, Leif could think of only one thing: what would Rebellious' foal be like?

Passing Carroll's farm, he saw Combat First in his paddock. Leif swerved the truck over to the fence, stopped it and got out.

The big red stallion, running low, his mane flying, small head straight out, raced toward him.

Leif watched, fascinated. If Rebellious should have a foal like this horse— He put his hand cautiously through the square of woven wire to touch the black velvety nose, and couldn't help chuckling with delight at sight of Combat's sleek neck and the power in those long fine-boned legs.

"Hi, Guy," he breathed, rubbing up along Combat's nose. "How goes it?"

Combat snorted, then swerved and, with a high kick, streaked down the paddock.

Leif clung to the fence, his eyes on Combat, and his heart pounding.

Determinedly he turned around and leaped into the truck and started down the road toward Ike Waite's. Rebellious had been an old steeplechaser, he remembered Ike's saying. Well, then, having a foal like Combat was possible.

His head overflowing with plans, Leif drove through the wire gate and down to Ike's unpainted shack barn.

Ike came out of the battered doorway, still grinning, still licking his thin lips over the slick deal he'd pulled on Leif.

"You come for your mare?" he asked, bearing down on the your.

Leif shut his lips tight, nodding. The only thing that counted, he told himself, was to get Rebellious home. Safe in that little round pole corral. Safe and waiting for Combat's foal.

"She's over there," Ike said, turning a dirty thumb to the east of the barn. "I'm gittin' ready to go to Lethbridge." He grinned again. "Goin' to buy pigs with that money you let me save."

Leif crawled out of the cab.

Waite prodded again.

" If I do well with them pigs, I'll give you a shoat— maybe—" His rust-brown eyes crinkled with scornful amusement.

Leif flushed.

"Okay, Mr. Waite," he blurted out, incautiously. "And when Rebellious' colt takes the Stockman's race from Carroll and McCarty's best horses, I'll let you sit by me in the grandstand."

Waite's eyes fell unbelievingly on Leif, then narrowed at him.

"So that's what's been eating you?" he said. "That's what got you all riled up about my note?" Suddenly he leaned up against the truck and laughed till tears pushed the dust down his lean face. When he could get his breath, he took Leif's arm and led him with long awkward steps through the barn and out to a board corral at the back.

Over by the side farthest from the barn, and munching dirty brown wheat straw from a rick, stood a scrub stallion. Black and not much bigger than a cayuse pony.

"There's the sire of the colt Rebellious will foal," Waite said, with curling lips. "If she has any—she's so ornery she'll most likely die an' the foal along with her."

Leif looked from Waite to the black scrub stallion, then back to Waite. Something within him set like cement. He felt red crawling up his neck.

"I don't believe it," he snapped. "You'd be crazy to let her have a foal by this, this—scrub."

He turned and walked through the barn and out to

take Rebellious' halter rope that had been flung over her thin long neck.

Ike, who'd followed, just chuckled and watched Leif. "So you think I'd be crazy?" he asked. "Well," he chuckled again. "By the time you own Rebellious a week you'll see that I didn't have anything to do with it— Rebellious does as she pleases."

All Leif wanted to do was get Rebellious in the trailer. He took the rope over the mare's long head and started leading her toward the trailer.

"Hold on—that halter's mine," Waite said. He took the rope from Leif's hands and shucked it over the mare's head.

"Okay," Leif nodded, bringing a new red-leather one with a long white cotton rope from the trailer and slipping it on Rebellious.

"Now, come on Rebellious," he coaxed, urging the mare toward the ramp of the trailer.

But it seemed as though a demon possessed the mare. She started backing up away from the trailer ramp.

Leif pulled.

She backed faster.

Waite from the distance doubled up with laughter and didn't make a move to help.

"That's what I've been tellin' you," he called.

Rebellious put on speed and, reaching the corral behind the barn, suddenly turned and with a quick agile bound cleared the fence and trotted over to stand by the scrub stallion.

"See?" Waite snickered.

Leif peered through the fence.

"You better name her colt Rebel, right now," Waite suggested, with another snicker. Suddenly, with long lean hands he opened the corral gate and, walking in beside the mare, pulled her ear down and whispered in it. Then taking her rope, and before the wide eyes of Leif, led her back to the edge of the trailer ramp. "There," Waite said, handing the rope to Leif. "Try again."

Leif said, "You lead her in."

Waite grinned and shook his head.

"And get rammed. Not me."

Leif took the rope and walked up the ramp.

The mare put her front feet on the boards. Then, with a wild lunge that knocked Leif flat and to one side, she leaped clean into the trailer and on over it. With a wild neigh, she raced to the gate, turned south and sped down the road, head up, tail flying.

Waite held his sides. Through his tears of laughter, he watched Leif climb to his feet.

"Don't worry," he jibed, at the concern in Leif's face. "She'll be okay—and you'll find her where there's something to eat."

"In my barn." Leif was hopeful, remembering the

new manger he'd built and stuffed with fragrant prairie hay.

But when he reached home and drove up to the barn, it was empty.

Leif gulped and, turning, drove the truck into the machine shed. Suddenly, walking out, he put his hand to his forehead and felt as though he might take off. For there, standing in the kitchen door, her neck stretched out, her soft lips closing on them, was Rebellious eating biscuits from Anna's hands.

"Biscuits—isn't she crazy?" Anna called, giggling.

Leif strode across the yard to them.

"But, they'll kill her," he protested.

"Leif, I like that. My biscuits!"

"I mean, they're swell, but a horse—"

He took Rebellious' halter rope from around her neck, and ran a hand along her side. Suddenly came that surge of hope within him. The mare'd run six miles and she seemed hardly breathing hard.

"Just have a colt, Rebellious," Leif whispered, trying to lead her toward the barn. "A little red colt with a satin skin and long legs and a heart as big as a bucket."

Rebellious took a dozen docile steps, softly nuzzling Leif's windbreaker, then with a flourish shook loose from Leif. This time, it was north to the end of the lot, then over the fence and into Mrs. Swanson's lettuce bed.

"Shoo! Shoo!" Mrs. Swanson's ample arms waved a broom at Rebellious. "My best winter lettuce!"

Leif leaped the fence and caught the mare's rope.

"I'll pay for the lettuce, Mrs. Swanson," he soothed.

"Yah—this is the beginning of more trouble," Mrs. Swanson's blond head nodded toward the mare. "She ain't machinery like what you know about, Leif."

Leif, leading the mare gingerly out of the garden and back to the corral gate before his barn, had to admit that Mrs. Swanson was right. But, a colt! Just let her give him a racing foal, and nothing else mattered.

He tried to lead her through the gate.

Rebellious agreed, stepping daintily through the big plank gate and over to the barn door. She nickered softly.

"Good girl," Leif breathed. "Now come on into the barn." He stepped across the sill with the rope in his hand.

"Hey!" Leif picked himself up from the dirt to see Rebellious standing out by the gate. He walked out to lead her once more to the barn door entrance.

To the entrance and no farther, would she step.

Leif tried for an hour to get her to go inside.

Rebellious just shook her head and stared longingly through the door at the brown hay.

"Start her up and run her in—pretend she's an I.H.C. tractor." Soren chuckled from outside the corral fence.

Leif, his face brick-red from exertion and determination, stared at Soren in disgust.

"She's got to be taken easy," he said, professionally. "If she doesn't want to go in, she can stay out."

"That's smart. Considerin' her sex. Well, it's goin' to rain and Big Chris said to gather up this junk." Soren walked across the yard to a stack of binder canvases.

Leif glanced at the sky. It was going to rain. He tried again to get Rebellious into the barn. Then he shut the door so she couldn't get in.

She promptly turned around and kicked at the door till splinters flew. Leif had to open it. Rebellious shook her head against the wind that sprang up with the smell of rain in the air.

Leif tried talking to her, as Waite had done. Rebellious listened, her soft eyes on the scudding clouds, but didn't budge.

Leif, too, studied the clouds.

"Going to be a three-day rain," he whispered, his lips tightening. "And, old girl, you've got to get inside!"

Rebellious chewed at a button on his jumper. But there was a look in her eyes.

Big Chris came by. He and Leif went into the barn and together they pulled on the mare's rope.

She leaned back.

"Enjoying it—tug of war," Big Chris grunted. "Here, I'll show her." He took a dally around the stall partition.

But Rebellious plainly considered that wasn't fair. Setting her weight, she leaned into the rope and gave a quick jerk back. A big plank sailed past Chris and Leif and on out the door.

Rebellious looked at it, switching her tail, then turned her head to stare east across Magrath's trees to a line of willows along the quicksanded canal bank. She looked back at Leif and shook her head, tossing the plank, and nickered softly.

"Take this plank off my rope," she seemed to say. "And give in."

Leif looked at Big Chris, then back to Rebellious.

"She wins," he said. "I'll feed her out here—bed her down."

Leif went on fixing her up for the night—scattering clean yellow wheat straw in a corner by the feed track, putting new prairie hay in the rack itself. He did everything he could think of for her.

And then after all his work and care Rebellious ran out on him. In the dark she left only a top pole off the side of the corral to show which way she had headed. For eleven days Leif looked for the mare every spare minute he had. She had vanished.

JUST before midnight on the eleventh night, Leif came softly into the bedroom. He'd been out for a last futile look around.

"Any luck?" Big Chris mumbled, turning over under the patchwork quilt. The wind came softly through the opened window, gently flapping the blind.

"No, but it's clearing," Leif said, undressing and crawling in beside Big Chris. He closed his eyes, and the next thing he knew, Leif heard the crazily jerking blind together with the sound of rain beating on the roof—torrents of it.

He jumped out of bed and rushed to close the window. "Pitch black—can't see a thing," he mumbled, dressing quickly.

His ears strained for a sound of Rebellious as he rushed down the stairs, into his slicker and out to the corral. She might have wandered back.

But no sound came, and the corral was empty—

With his heart turning over, Leif rushed through the gate and to the barn door, left open to welcome her. She was not there—

Leif swung around to stare out into the blackness, panic seized him. This was a wicked night and if she had foaled?

A flash of lightning lighted the way east leading toward the canal.

Somehow he knew Rebellious had done the worst possible thing—gone to the most dangerous place. He started in that direction.

"The crazy—" A groan escaped Leif, staring toward

the canal banks, slimy with quicksand. He ran sliding along the edge of the flooding stream. Past a clump of willows, past a little lean-to shed the canal inspector used for tools. No sign of the mare.

Leif stopped and called loudly above the dashing rain.

No answering nicker. Nothing but the lash of wind through the willows.

He called again. Then stopped, listening. Nothing. He started on.

Suddenly, from along the bank, came a faint nicker. Leif sprang toward it. Nothing but darkness.

He called again.

Again came the nicker, then silence.

But before that silence, Leif had found Rebellious. Head in the swirling canal water, too weak to raise it, she'd drowned.

By her side two shapes struggled in the mud there on the canal bank. Leif's heart all but stopped as he moved toward them.

"Rainboy," he said softly, helping the first gangling colt up the bank. A flash of lightning revealed the shiny wet body, the long back, the long slender legs, and slim head of a running colt. It was the boy's idea of what his horse should look like. Leif shouted aloud. Happiness overflowed within him.

But a second flash of lightning showed him something that pleased him less. For there, struggling in the mud

just beyond Rebellious' quiet body, stood a second colt.
A big rawboned colt, all legs with a big head and a red
furry body.

"Red!" burst from Leif, running down to help him.
"Big—" he added. "Big Red!" But the brawny colt that
obstinately turned from his help to plunge into the canal
and try to swim ruggedly for the opposite bank was not
the horse he had dreamed of. He seemed homely. Leif
looked at this colt and saw again Ike Waite's scrub.

Racing along the bank to help him, Leif wished
there'd been only one—the smooth foal he'd found first.
The colt he felt had the makings of a runner.

And as he stooped to give a hand to Big Red who'd
been forced to come back to his side of the bank after all,
Leif's worry increased. For the colt nudged his hands
away, climbed the bank and stood defiantly, dripping,
but square on his own knobby legs.

Here was trouble, Leif sensed. It looked as if this one
was Rebellious all over again. Dutifully, Leif took hold of
the little rebel and herded him along with Rainboy into
the shed and out of the storm. But he couldn't help wishing
as he hovered the two colts there, drying them with an old
sack, while he waited for daylight and Big Chris to come
and help him, that Big Red hadn't been born. Rainboy,
the quiet little guy that seemed to have Combat written
all over him, was the one to whom he would devote
himself.

CHAPTER 3

The Character

IN THE MONTHS that followed Big Red made a reputation for himself. It began from the moment Leif, with Big Chris helping, got the two colts to the barn door. The rain had stopped and a bright morning sun brought out the sheen of Rainboy's coat—and the dull shagginess of Big Red's.

"We'll put 'em in the barn," Leif innocently said.

Rainboy walked over the sill and into the second stall on the right.

Big Red came as far as the door, then stubbornly braced his gangling body and wouldn't step over the wooden sill.

"Come on, don't be a dope," Leif urged, giving the colt's rump a shove.

Big Red's heels lashed past Leif's shoulder.

Big Chris promptly picked Big Red up and dropped him into the first stall by the door and next to Rainboy.

"Don't get tough with me." He grinned.

Big Red promptly leaped for the manger, getting his forelegs over the plank and dangling.

"He'll kill himself!" Anna cried from the barn door. "The big beauty!" It was plain which colt she liked.

"Let him," Leif retorted. But he couldn't let the little guy hang there. He took him down.

Big Red did it all over again.

In the end, Big Red won out and finally took his place in the pole corral.

Feeding the colts was the same kind of story.

Rainboy took his milk from a bottle through the finger of a rubber glove fashioned into a nipple. He took it peaceably, licking his lips for more, and staring gently into the next stall back, where Spot, the cow stood.

"He's a nice little guy," said Old Man Kyne, who'd brought Spot down from his farm on the ridge. "He'll get to be a race horse some day—beat McCarty's and Carroll's colts. And my cow will help—"

"It surely was swell of you to bring her down, Mr. Kyne," Leif said.

He took a second bottle of milk out to Big Red.

"Here," he said, sticking the nipple in between the colt's teeth.

Big Red promptly bit the rubber finger off. The milk spilled down his bony jaws. He just stood looking off toward the mountains.

At last, after two more nipples and a scuffle with a

bucket, trying to make him drink from it, they had to lead old Spot out and force her to submit to Big Red's suckling her.

"Tsch—tsch!" Old man Kyne went away, shaking his head. "What a character—what a disposition!"

So Big Red got the name around Magrath of being a character. It plagued Leif. Through the winter, with his constant efforts to develop Rainboy, and his still more constant efforts to keep Big Red from freezing to death in the corral.

Then, on into the spring, with the rush of setting up seeders and plows, and the countless jobs around the I.H.C. agency. With Soren, always smiling, always busy, and Big Chris, it seemed, always away—out among the farmers trying to sell machinery.

"Why can't you act like Rainboy?" Leif demanded one day. "See, he's eating his carrots?"

Big Red let his winter carrot sag limply from his lips, then fall to the ground. He shoved his nose in the air, and suddenly ran at the side of the corral, took a huge leap, cleared it, and brought up just outside the kitchen door.

Anna came out, laughing, and holding a pan of snowy biscuits.

"You great big beautiful—" she crooned, leaning her blonde head down along his big red one. "You like my biscuits better than anything."

Leif, watching Big Red eat one from Anna's white hand, then another, shook his head in disgust and went back into the barn to study Rainboy. He ran his hand along his sleek bay body, and on down his slim legs to the pasterns.

"Boy!" He breathed, his imagination taking fire. And his mind, for the moment, free of Big Red, and fixed on the future when Rainboy would swing into the lead at the Stockman's against the best that Carroll and McCarty had to offer.

But a squeal from Anna brought him running to the barn door. Big Red had eaten all of the pan of biscuits and was crowding through the kitchen door looking hungrily for more.

Leif, with a groan, walked quickly across the yard, took hold of Big Red's halter and led him back into the corral. Then he shut the gate.

But the corral wouldn't hold Big Red.

Nothing seemed to hold him. And nothing could keep him out of trouble and from interfering with Leif's precious time with Rainboy. For with the advance of summer, came the trouble with Mr. McKibbey, the Boy Rangers' leader.

McKibbey came through the machine yard and over to Leif, who was working on a binder.

"I tell you, I won't have it." Mr. McKibbey turned

earnest blue eyes on Leif, and straightened his lath-like body the full six feet three.

"But, what harm's Big Red doing—the boys are crazy about him." Leif, half-heartedly argued. "And he's a good Ranger."

"Indeed?" McKibbey's long face became thin and pained-looking. "Can he build a fire with sticks—or make a bed?"

Leif swallowed a snicker, then suddenly sympathised with Mr. McKibbey.

"No," he said, sadly. "I guess not. He can't do anything but get in trouble."

His words were scarcely out before he heard shouts of laughter coming from down the street.

Anna Larson's brother Jimmy, Ronald Swanson, the storekeeper's son, George Culp's son, Walter, and half a dozen others hove into view. At their head, marched Big Red.

"Looky, Leif," they called, filing across the lot to him. "A new member."

Leif couldn't help smiling, even above the anxiety he felt for Mr. McKibbey. For Big Red did look funny. Leif took the Ranger hat from between Big Red's ears and handed it back to the Ranger head.

"I'm sorry, Mr. McKibbey," he said. "But, I do the best I can. I'll try to keep Big Red at home after this." He led the red colt over to the corral and shoved him inside.

But, in the end, Big Red became a special Ranger.

"You see," Mr. McKibbey admitted a week later, "the boys have lost interest in the Rangers." He picked at a slat, while his faded blue eyes went out past Leif's binder to the sun glistening on snowy Ahern Pass. "I sort of miss him myself," he finally admitted.

Leif nodded. He had to agree that Big Red got under your skin. Twice he'd been on the verge of selling the big clown to Culp who wanted a pony for Walter. But both times Big Red had saved himself.

The first time he'd kicked over a box of machine parts, discovering for Leif a valuable part to the binder he'd thought was gone. Again, he'd neighed and raised a fuss in the night, getting Leif grumbling from bed to come out and find Rainboy all but hung on his halter—a loose spike had caught it.

With his knees trembling and wondering what he'd done if Rainboy, his hope for the Stockman's, had been killed, Leif had put his head along Big Red's there in the dark and whispered, "You've earned your keep. I'll never sell you now. Never!"

Big Red had reached around and torn the top button clean off Leif's leather jumper and swallowed it. So now, Leif nodded understandingly to Mr. McKibbey and went and opened the corral gate.

Big Red loped through the gate and down the road with Mr. McKibbey's tall angular frame following.

So Big Red became a Ranger in good standing.

They were taking a trip up into the Rockies. They'd go up across Ahern and down to the great grassy Hidden Valley and maybe over to Lost Island, that two-mile-long wooded strip in the middle of Waterton Lake.

"He'll ride in the truck," Mr. McKibbey explained above the roar of the tractor Leif was tuning up for George Culp. "We gave him a trial ride. He seemed to understand he'd have to be good if he was to go—"

"And taking in everything, I'll bet you," Leif added. He was to remember this remark when Big Red became an outcast—a hunted colt for stealing a band of mares.

Mr. McKibbey nodded. "He'll be okay."

Leif nodded. It would give him two full weeks of peace with Rainboy. He could get on with his training.

"That's swell," he said. "And, good luck!"

The next morning, standing with Rainboy's halter rope in his hands, he watched the big red truck go rumbling by. The front was loaded with bed rolls and food, but in the back, and surrounded by shouting boys, stood Big Red.

Seeing Rainboy, Big Red whinnied.

Rainboy glanced once at him, then turned and dropped his soft velvety nose to the water trough.

"Rainboy's a sissy!" screamed Walter Culp. "A sissy!"
The others in the truck took it up. And they all rolled
in a cloud of dust, down the road and toward the snow-
laden Rockies to the west.

Leif turned back to Rainboy, ashamed of a slightly
guilty wish that Big Red might like the mountains. Per-
haps he'd stay there on the big grassy plain behind Ahern
Pass, or maybe on Lost Island?

This too, he was to remember contritely with Big Red
a hunted horse and himself a frightened lad looking for
him.

But now, he turned his attention to Rainboy. Getting
out a long rope, he tied it through Rainboy's halter, then
let the colt trot around him.

Carroll came by. Big Jim Carroll with his ten-gallon
hat and belly-laugh.

"What is this, Leif? Treason?" he joshed, pulling his
coupe up to the fence and getting out.

Leif's heart bumped. He had trouble keeping calm,
watching Rainboy's fleet legs as he scampered the circle
around him.

"Don't get worried, Mr. Carroll," he said. "He's just
a colt I picked up." Briefly, he explained to Jim about
Rebellious and about the twin colts.

"Where's the other one?" Jim asked, glancing around.

Leif laughed.

"He's a Ranger—gone to the mountains with the kids."

Carroll's big mouth sagged open. He took off his hat and scratched his head, then looked at McCarty coming along on a bay saddle horse.

"Say that again—slower," he demanded.

McCarty rode up, and what Leif had to say was lost. McCarty walked over to take Rainboy's halter rope. He ran a slim wiry hand down his legs.

"What have you here?" he snapped.

Leif told him Rainboy's pedigree.

"Nice conformation," McCarty nodded, examining Rainboy's straight back. "Want to sell him, Leif? Give you five hundred."

Leif's throat went dry. Five hundred—the amount of Waite's note and then some. It was a great temptation and with Big Chris crowded plenty.

His face flushed red, his hands were cold. He stuttered, and looked at Carroll, then at McCarty. Then it all came out—how he'd planned on taking the Stockman's Race when Rainboy grew up.

"So—that's it?" McCarty snapped.

He looked at Carroll, then at Leif, and suddenly the three of them burst out laughing.

Leif took the plunge. "I don't suppose you'd consider a third horse running?" he said.

For a full minute, no one spoke.

Then Carroll turned to Leif.

"Combat Third'll be ready next year. I'm not worried," he said.

McCarty's steel-blue eyes shut a little tighter.

"I like competition—some competition," he shot Carroll a meaning glance. "And with that colt Thunderbolt—" He turned a dry smile to Leif. "We'll be looking for you, Leif."

McCarty wasn't like Carroll. He was a tight-lipped bachelor, always on the prod. He cared for nothing in the world except a good horse and someone named Auntie McCarty whom nobody around here had ever seen.

The two men walked away in the direction of Swanson's store. Friendly, but rivals.

"So," Leif pulled Rainboy's sleek head to him. "Hear that, guy?" he asked excitedly. "It's settled. We've got to start training for the Stockman's Race."

But before he could get Rainboy for more than two days to himself, here came the Ranger truck back, loaded with wailing kids.

"He's gone," they told Leif, crowding tearfully around him. "He jumped into the lake and swam across to Lost Island. We swum him back and he got sore. That night, he pulled out."

Mr. McKibbey climbed stiffly down from the truck.

Leif looked at him and sensed that another year's scouting with Big Red in the troop would be the finish of him.

"I don't know where he could have gone," McKibbey faltered. "I really don't—we sent trackers."

"But, but he was too good a Ranger. He lost himself," Jimmy Larson wailed. "You find him, Leif. You just have to."

Leif, thinking of his interrupted training of Rainboy, nodded slowly. "I'll try," he finally said.

Four days' search, right in the busiest time at the agency, resulted in no Big Red. When Leif got back, he found that Rainboy had lost weight. Soren had mixed too much condition powder in his food ration. He was a sick colt.

Leif stayed up nights with him. Rainboy under blankets was still shaking with chills and fever. He stood there with his eyes closed, and Leif suddenly felt very low.

He tried to get Rainboy to eat. The colt turned his head away from the mash. He sniffed at the water, then refused to drink.

Another day passed.

Another night, with no change in Rainboy's condition. Except that he was thinner and weaker.

"Tomorrow, we'll have to put you in a sling," Leif said, coming slowly back to sit on a stool beside Rainboy. He leaned up against the stall and closed his eyes.

The sound of ravenous eating wakened him.

"Big Red!" Leif was ashamed of himself for the tears that suddenly filled his eyes. He sprang up and walked over to the colt. "A scratch—looks like a cat. A big cat!" He whistled, putting a hand on Big Red's flinching shoulder.

Big Red went on gulping the mash.

Rainboy nickered softly, and swung his head up and down, licking his lips.

"Hungry?" Leif bolted to the house for more mash and held it for Rainboy to eat. "Boy!" He turned to Big Red, now standing staring at the lantern. "You've saved Rainboy's life—you came back just in time."

Big Red turned and walked out of the barn and over to his rack in the corral and began munching hay.

Leif, watching, knew a great weight had been lifted from him. The winter coming would soon pass. The winter during which he could nurse Rainboy back to health, study him, feed him properly and prepare him for the spring breaking to saddle—for the racing he would get as a two-year-old.

CHAPTER 4

The Striped Pussy

BUT IT WAS the following May before Leif could begin the breaking of Rainboy. There had been so much to do at the agency—binders to set up in the fall, then the winter snows blocking any training, and with spring, the rush of seeders for the wheat planting.

Then, one sunny May morning, Leif found himself in the barn door and ready for action.

Big Red frisked around the corral, nose down, teeth about half an inch from the waving tail of the black barn cat. Every once in a while, he'd clamp down, lift the cat in the air to hear him yowl. They went out of sight around the corner of the barn this way.

Leif grinned, but turned to go in beside Rainboy.

But before he'd more than crossed the sill, Carroll drove up to the corral with a flourish and got out of his coupe dragging a sweet little racing saddle.

"Here, Leif," he said gruffly. "Put this on that slick guy—" He motioned past Leif to Rainboy standing slim and straight and a full two years old in his stall.

41

Leif, thankful that Big Red had gone from sight—the big clown—could hardly speak with pleased surprise. He reddened, then took hold of the saddle.

"What a beauty," he said. "I was wondering what I would do for a saddle—thanks, Mr. Carroll."

"It's the least I can do—seeing I'm going to take the race from you. And of course from McCarty, too."

Leif turned toward Rainboy.

"Well, so long," Jim said, making it to his car.

"Aren't you going to see me saddle up?" Leif protested. He really wanted Jim around. There was something swell about him. And maybe Leif could get some ideas on Rainboy. Maybe Carroll'd make the guy cut up a little bit. Not act so docile. Some folks said it was bad luck for a colt not to buck a little the first time he was ridden.

"Nope, sorry," Jim said, kicking over his engine. "Got to mooch—say, Leif, where's that Ranger colt. Not leading a troop of his own yet, is he?"

"No, he's around. He's swell, but no runner."

"Well, so long," Jim shoved his car in gear and wove past a plow and a left-over seeder, then out of the yard.

Leif walked in beside Rainboy, got a currycomb and groomed him from the tips of his ears to the bottoms of his slim shiny hind legs. He roughed Rainboy up, hoping to get him a little on the prod.

Soren, fat and jolly, came in to stand behind Leif.

"No use, Leif," he said, shaking his head. "You can't

get that guy on the prod. He's good—too good to be true."

Leif turned to stare at Soren.

"Skip it," he said, but his heart beat a little faster. "He's okay. He'll show his spirit on the track."

Soren snorted, and turned to face Anna in the doorway.

"Oh, Leif," she breathed, her blue eyes sparkling. "You going to break Rainboy today."

"Break him, humph!" Soren shrugged. "He's broke now. I bet you he won't even crow-hop when Leif gets on him."

"Soren!" Anna's eyes fell sternly on the old Swede.

Leif tossed the saddle on Rainboy's back. How well it fitted him. He cinched it around Rainboy's slim body, and his breath came fast with excitement.

"You guys'll see something when I clip off a record half-mile," Leif breathed.

"Today?" Anna gasped.

"'Course not," Soren exploded. "He's got to break him, first. Then, the running begins, maybe?"

Leif tightened the cinch, his breath coming a little faster with hope. Most colts would have lunged a bit, or humped into a knot with the cinch. Rainboy just stood like a veteran.

Big Red came back around the corner, still trailing the cat. At the door, he clamped down on the tail before him and hoisted the cat into the air.

Soren snickered.

"I hope he knows his cats. Some day he'll get hold of that striped one—you know—that lives down behind the machine shed."

"Soren — he wouldn't!" Anna exclaimed. "That skunk!"

Soren shrugged. "Maybe not—anyway, I hope not." They climbed to the corral fence.

Leif bridled Rainboy. The colt took the straight racing bit like a gentleman.

"You'd lose a finger bridling Big Red that way," Soren said from the fence-top. "Hurry up and get on. It won't last a minute. It's too e-a-s-y."

Leif led Rainboy out into the center of the pole corral. A slight breeze blew from the west. A dry breeze, when the farmers needed rain to sprout the wheat they'd already planted. If there was another failure this year, and collections for Big Chris became any worse—

"Rainboy," he whispered, tossing the reins over the colt's head. "A lot depends on what you do in the next half hour."

Rainboy looked off to the Rockies, his big brown eyes steady, his body shivering slightly. Leif could see the play of muscles under the skin of his shoulders, and confidence returned to him. That's the way Combat had looked at the Fair—trembling at the post.

He gathered up the reins, then, taking a deep breath, eased into the saddle.

Big Red hoisted the cat in the air

For a long moment he sat there waiting for a protest from the colt—a lunge or two. Anything.

Nothing happened. Rainboy just stood looking calmly off into the distance.

"Whooppee!" Soren whispered, sarcastically.

"Soren!" Anna, sitting primly, chided. "Just because he's a gentleman—oh!" She jumped as Big Red, with a flash of his body, swept out the gate and by her.

Rainboy didn't bat an eye. Leif, feeling funny inside, turned his head sideways, running him around the corral. Rainboy took it all in good form.

"Oh, he's a beauty," Anna cried, clapping her white hands. "All the people clap for him when he goes up the track."

"Yeah, up. But coming back they can't find him, he's so far behind the winner." Soren glumly got off the fence and walked toward the red machine shed.

Leif tried another idea. He took Rainboy out of the corral and down the mile road leading to McCarty's. He poked Rainboy. He even resorted to running his thumbs along the colt's neck—a thing that sets any horse crazy.

The colt just shook his slim head and turned questioning eyes back to Leif's.

"I beg your pardon, but you're insulting me," they seemed to say.

Leif, desperate, sweat running down his face, set off across the wind-swept field.

"A jack rabbit—" he prayed. "Anything to upset Rainboy—get a rise out of him. Carroll said it had to be done."
And Jim Carroll knew.

But a "jack" didn't do it. For the big brown one, with
ears like a donkey, that leaped from behind a buckbrush
bush, hardly broke Rainboy's stride.

Leif gulped.

A tumble weed rolled past, getting in Rainboy's slim
legs. The average colt would have thrown a fit. Rainboy
just stopped and waited for Leif to dismount and break
him out of it.

Leif gave up, then. He remounted Rainboy and rode
him slowly back across the prairie and to the barn.

"Whooppee!" jibed Soren from the machine-shed
door.

"Don't you mind," Anna said, coming from the
kitchen. "Here, Rainboy." She extended a cold biscuit.

Rainboy ignored it, and Anna, swinging around to
throw it away, suddenly screamed and held her nose.

"No Big Red!" she protested. "Not that kitty—"

Soren's chuckle sounded.

Leif turned in his saddle to watch.

Here came Big Red, nose down, teeth about six inches
from the waving plumy tail of an outraged skunk. They
came straight toward the barn.

"Oh, do something. He'll pick him up by the tail,
and—oo-oh!" Anna wailed.

"There's nothing to do," Soren called, then ducked inside the shed door.

Leif, petrified, sat Rainboy.

Fifty feet, thirty feet, twenty, and through the gate came the big red horse, nose down, and a clownish tilt to his neck.

"See me, folks," his manner seemed to say. Then, suddenly, when he was less than ten feet from Rainboy, he picked the skunk up by the tail and waved him aloft. He waited calmly while an overpowering odor settled like a fog over the place.

Suddenly, Rainboy's delicate pink nostrils distended. His neck bowed in outrage. His back humped and with a bawl of anger, he crow-hopped out of the corral and on out through the machine yard.

Leif, clinging to him, fighting to stay on, knew a sweet peace. He let the colt buck along the road for a quarter of a mile, then let him straighten to a run, to a trot, and with gentle hands neck reined him around and back to the barn.

As he rode into the corral, something of a sob came to his throat.

Anna put it into words.

"Well, Big Red did it again," she said.

"The big clown." Soren nodded, coming from the shed.

"Yeah," Leif said, unsaddling Rainboy and leading

him into his stall. "Where is the big guy?" He could
have kissed him right then.

Soren motioned toward the canal.

"He went that way," he said. "And the skunk went
this way." He motioned toward a hole under the west
corner of the machine shed.

Leif took the road down to the canal. Near the little
tool house, he stopped a moment by a mound of dirt that
was Rebellious' grave.

Suddenly, he heard a big splash in the direction of the
dam.

"Big Red!" he exclaimed. With a quick run along the
canal bank, he made it to where Big Red swam out in the
center of the lake. Throwing off his clothes, he dived in
and swam with powerful overhand strokes out to the
horse.

"Old boy," he breathed, swimming alongside the
horse. "Thank you."

Big Red snorted. He swerved and tried to toss water
over Leif's slim brown body.

"You've earned the right to be broken, too," Leif said,
dodging. "And tomorrow, we'll do it."

Big Red shook his head and struck out for the opposite
bank, made it up the side and, mane flying, big glistening
body leaping, disappeared from sight.

Leif swam a few minutes, then thoughtfully back to

pull on his blue denim shirt and cords. Breaking Rainboy had been easy—too easy. But riding Big Red would be something else again.

"Tomorrow," he whispered, taking the road back to town. "And it'll be plenty tough."

CHAPTER 5

A Close Call

NEXT MORNING breaking Big Red didn't look any easier. It was Saturday, and Leif, hot and sweating, stood inside the pole corral preparing to catch Big Red.

Stacked in the middle of the corral was an old stock saddle, a navajo blanket and a bridle with a curved bit. The top pole was lined with excited shouting Boy Rangers. Big Red stood by his hayrick, eying Leif with his head tossing up and down.

"Come on, guy," Leif said softly, coiling his lariat for a throw at Big Red's tossing mane. "Slip into this noose— let's get this over with. I've to get on with Rainboy."

Big Red snorted as Leif approached. Horse and boy paid no attention to a dark hawk-faced man getting out of the cream coupe which had pulled up in front of the I.H.C. office.

The rope sang out.

Big Red dodged it with a quick sinuous movement of head and neck. Then he ran across the corral, snorting. The boys whooped and yelled, taunting Leif.

"Big Red'll throw you so high the birds'll build nests in your hair!"

Leif grinned and coiling his rope made another pass at the scornful red head.

Big Red thought it was a game. He dodged, ran headlong at the side of the corral, then pulled up short, his eyes shining, his mane flying.

Dirt flew up on the delighted Rangers.

"Yipee!" yelped Jimmy Larsen.

"Hey, guy!" Ronnie Swanson called. "This pole's too light to hold you."

The dark man coming across the yard checked his walk at sight of the big red colt's powerful run. The soft play of his muscles. The man's eyes, which were small and mean, flashed evilly.

"Boy, that's a horse I can make a killer out of," he muttered, with a low smirk. "I'll do this boy out of him." He moved on toward the dusty corral.

Leif coiled his rope once more. He wished things would move a little faster, with Rainboy in the barn, waiting to be trained.

He made another pass.

Big Red gave the boys their money's worth. He dodged and shied, wheeled and kicked his heels in the sunshine, then, stopping a few feet from Leif, neighed out across the town to the distant foothills.

Soren came along to poke his head through the fence.

"That colt's growing up," he said, with a shake of his head. "Maybe he'll make for those hills, pretty soon."

Leif wiped the sweat from his forehead and flung the rope at Big Red for another try. The colt stayed just out of its reach.

Suddenly, a voice came through the corral poles.

"Put up your rope. I'll give you a hundred dollars for that cayuse—just as he stands."

Leif wheeled around. Hard up as he and Big Chris were, a hundred dollars sounded pretty good.

"A hundred?" he repeated, eying the stranger.

"He's got a mean face," Soren whispered, coming through the gate and up to Leif. Scratching his head, he added, "Where have I seen it before—some place."

"Leif, you wouldn't sell Big Red?" came Anna's shocked voice. She'd been standing quietly admiring Big Red through it all, and her firm hands left biscuit flour marks on the corral pole as she gripped it in agitated concern.

An angry shocked murmur ran along the top pole.

"Beat it, guy!" Walter Culp mumbled under his breath, fixing the man with somber brown eyes. "Leif don't want to sell no colt to you."

Leif, to keep from having to answer, coiled his rope and made another throw, settling the loop over that weaving bobbing head.

Big Red stopped stiff-legged as the rope tightened on

his neck. He bucked, then wheeled and catching the
rope under his heels, kicked till it was free. It was a show
for him and the boys, who whooped and laughed and
taunted Leif.

"He'll make you pull leather. You'll choke that saddle-
horn to death."

It gave the dark man a chance to come persuasively in
to stand by Leif.

"Make it a hundred and a quarter," he said, his eyes
fascinated by Big Red's power. "I've a use for that colt."

Anna's choked voice came from outside the corral.
Then her honey-colored braids caught the sun as she
turned and raced for her kitchen.

Jimmy Larsen and Walter Culp kicked the corral pole
under their feet.

"Beat it, guy," they said, soberly.

The dark man smiled at Leif, including him in a
grown-up way.

"These kids," his smile said. "They'll forget the colt
over night." He led the way to Rainboy's stall.

And Leif, proud as punch of Rainboy, followed.

"What have you here?" the man asked.

Leif told him about Rainboy.

The man whistled softly and made man-to-man talk
with Leif.

"I'll bet you're in a hurry to start training. No wonder
with Jim Carroll's colt Combat III coming along. He's

running the six furlongs in a minute and a quarter now."

Leif gulped. And here he hadn't more than got a saddle on Rainboy.

"What about McCarty?" he asked.

"Oh, he's doing all right," the man said. "He's got a sorrel colt that steps plenty fast—won't give any time. You know how tight-lipped McCarty is. But his colt's running sweet."

"And here I'm held up with this big clown," Leif told himself. Once more, he walked out to Big Red, and succeeded in getting the colt cornered, bridled and a handkerchief over his eyes.

Big Red shook it off, eying Leif. His coat was sleek with sweat now, and a deep red. He looked up at the row of boys and shook his head, whinnying. It brought out the scar along his neck.

"Scar?" The man exclaimed, turning to Leif.

"A cat—when he was a yearling. Up in the mountains," Leif said, once more adjusting the blindfold, and this time managing to get the saddle on Big Red's straight-coupled back.

The man held his breath, then trying to keep from making his voice too eager to buy, said "That colt's a lot of horse. I'll give you one hundred and fifty—spot cash."

Without thinking, he walked over to touch Big Red, and the next minute picked himself up from the ground.

Just enough to knock him flat

Big Red had swung his body just enough to knock him flat. The saddle tumbled to the ground.

The boys chortled with glee. Derisive catcalls came from them.

"G'wan," they yelled, secure in numbers. "Roll y'er hoop, guy."

The man stooped to brush his dirty pants, his face a brick red, his thin lips a straight angry line.

"Make it one seventy-five," he snarled, his hands working spasmodically. "I've a use for that horse—"

Soren moved distractedly around the corral, his rolypoly back humped over.

"Where—where have I seen that guy?" He mumbled. "I've got to remember—"

Leif whispered, "One hundred and seventy-five dollars —it's a lot of money." It would give Big Chris something to run on, even if he kept out fifty for training expenses of Rainboy. He picked up his saddle and blanket, and managed to get the blanket on Big Red's back, once more.

The colt promptly humped his back and with two well-placed jumps landed it right around Jimmy Larsen's neck.

The Rangers went crazy with laughter. "That's the boy, Big Red," they cheered.

Leif walked over to pick the blanket from Larsen's

hands. He could hear Anna, from her kitchen, rattling biscuit pans as he walked back and once more put the blanket atop Big Red's back.

Big Red didn't budge. It was plain that he wanted something new.

Leif gently lifted the saddle and laid it gently on the quiet back. And the next instant, his eyes followed it sailing over the corral fence.

The dark man gasped. In spite of his anger, it was plain to Leif that he was knocked for a loop with desire for Big Red.

"Two hundred," the man said. "And right here—come on. After all, he can't run. He's keeping you from training Rainboy. And what have you after you get him ridden—provided you do—but a good saddle horse that'll maybe bring you around seventy-five bucks?"

He waved the green bills in the air all the time Leif was bringing the saddle back and placing it once more on Big Red's back.

"Naw—don't take it, Leif. Don't take it," chorused the boys. They were leaning forward on their elbows. And a sort of panic made them huddle together. Jimmy Larsen's freckles stood out clear, above the strain on his face.

Soren still paced the corral, muttering, "That guy's a bad actor—if I could only remember him?"

Leif buckled the cinch around Big Red's belly. Anger filled him. He was a plain sap to turn down two hundred dollars for a seventy-five-dollar horse.

"Come on, man to man, Leif," the man urged. "You have a year's training expenses coming up on Rainboy. "I'll make it two hundred and twenty-five."

Leif straightened, and swallowed.

The man pressed the money toward him.

"Come on," he urged, staring around at the buildings needing paint. "I guess your Dad can use the money—the machinery business with the drought isn't what it used to be."

Leif felt the sweat start to come out on his forehead. He pulled the cinch till it touched Big Red's lean belly. The big guy waited till Leif tightened it just enough to hold the saddle for a good show. Then he really went to work.

His bucking was a circus for the boys. He crow-hopped, swapped ends, then reared straight into the sunshine, making himself into a gleaming column of fighting horseflesh. Dropping to all fours, he went into a fit of straight powerful bucking.

The saddle cinch broke and flew past the dodging man standing beside Leif in the center of the corral.

"Man, oh, man!" His excitement got away from him. Incautiously, he reached for Leif. And in his hand lay two hundred and fifty dollars in bills. "It's my last offer," he said. "I need that horse and I'll pay—"

In the silence that followed, no one spoke.

Soren had come to a stop by the barn door, his face vacant looking. His usually smiling mouth sagged at the corners.

Leif felt a gone feeling at the pit of his stomach. Automatically, he walked into the barn and got another cinch, fastened it on the saddle, then put the saddle back on Big Red's back. He led him over to the dark man, his heart racing, his eyes once more fixed on that money—

Big Red just stood, blowing gently, his big black plume tail waving in the slight breeze.

"I don't know—" Leif whispered. "I don't know—"

Suddenly, without seeming to be able to stop the man, he felt the money being stuffed into his leather jumper pocket. The reins of Big Red's bridle started to leave his hands as the man's thin wiry hands tugged at them.

Then, he decided numbly, it was all over. It must be all over. He'd sold Big Red.

A sob ran along the fence. Ten pairs of stricken eyes were fixed hopelessly on Leif.

He couldn't move. His hand ran out to touch Big Red's soft nose, while icy fingers clutched at his midriff.

Then suddenly on the air came the odor of hot biscuits.

Big Red's nose went up. His head swung sharply

toward Anna, in a red and white gingham dress, coming across the yard with a gleaming pan of brown-topped biscuits in her big firm hands.

With a flip of his head, Big Red jerked his reins free from the stranger and flipped them across his neck. He ran toward the fence, gathered himself into a mighty knot of muscle, cleared the fence with a sailing leap, and hitting the ground outside, ran over to take a biscuit from Anna's hands and eat it ravenously.

"Big Red." Anna sobbed. "Big Red." Her hands kept feeding him more biscuits.

Leif hardly knew what happened next.

The boys were down around him and the stranger. A sort of urgency seemed to come into the air. They all moved toward the street and the man's car. The money got back into his hands, then into his pocket just before he opened the door and slid under the wheel.

"A sissy horse—likes biscuits," his lips said.

"Yeah, a sissy that eats biscuits," the boys chorused. "You don't want a horse like that. Sure you don't. So long, mister."

The man drove away, wiping his forehead, and batting dazed eyes.

Leif found that he'd said the words along with the boys, and that the knot had left his stomach.

Suddenly behind him came Soren's voice. "That guy," he said, triumphantly. "I remember him now. He's an outlaw maker—buys horses and makes them rodeo killers."

He stopped, grinning foolishly at the derisive laughter from the boys.

"Fine time to remember," they jibed, laughing some more. Then they trooped over to Big Red, with Leif following.

Without thinking of anything but Rainboy, Leif climbed aboard Big Red, and started him toward the barn.

"Looky," the boys shouted. "Leif's on Big Red. He's breaking him to ride, and Big Red likes it!"

Leif came to, grinning. It was a fact. The big red colt had done all the bucking he wanted. And he seemed to savvy that this was the sort of thing expected of a two-year-old.

Leif rode him past the barn to see that Rainboy was okay, then down the road the full mile toward McCarty's ranch. Tomorrow, he'd stake it off into quarters, then give Rainboy his first workout.

He rode Big Red back, unsaddled him and put him out to eat some hay at his feed rack. Then he came in to stand again by Rainboy.

"You'll show Carroll and McCarty," he whispered, slapping Rainboy's sleek round thigh. "You're going to be a flash—make Dad that two thousand dollars. Pull this agency out of the hole."

Rainboy just munched his hay, wiggling a fly from his right ear and standing quietly. The perfect gentleman.

Leif, unconscious of the disaster ahead, closed the barn door and walked toward the little white house.

CHAPTER 6

Disastrous Race

IN THE DAYS that followed, Leif was more sure than ever that Rainboy was the answer to everything. He staked out the mile road in quarters—a green flag at the first quarter, a white one at the second, and a red one at the finish.

At first, he didn't time the sleek bay colt. Just ran him the quarter every morning for a week, then the half for two weeks, and finally the full distance.

The day he'd finished the full mile for the first time, Jim Carroll met him as he rode slowly back to the barn.

"Some colt," Jim said, as Leif circled him, cooling Rainboy out. "Some colt! You've really got me worried, lad." His big red face looked up at Leif's. "Do you know what he did that mile in—I had a watch on him from start to finish?"

Leif's heart bumped his ribs. His Dad had him worried, and the weather. No rain. And the wheat crop almost a failure.

"No, what?" He asked in a stifled voice.

"1:40," Carroll replied. "A dead-heat time with my colt, Combat Third."

Leif could hardly speak. "That was fast."

"What—what about McCarty's colt, Thunderbolt?" Leif asked.

"Oh, that plow horse," Carroll waved a sunburned hand. "He'll get in in time for bacon and eggs in the Stockman's race next fall."

Leif walked Rainboy into his stall and tied him up.

"I don't know," he said, coming back to Carroll. "I heard he was pretty fast."

Carroll got up to climb back into his car.

"Leif," he said, leaning out. "How'd you like to make it a three-way race for two year old's on Dominion Day, July 1, at my ranch track. It's a sort of preliminary for next fall. Your colt, mine and that plow horse of Mc-Carty's?"

Leif felt a warm flood rush through him. He took hold of the window of Carroll's car to keep steady.

"Why, that's great," he said. "That's really great, Mr. Carroll."

Carroll kicked over his engine.

"Okay, it's settled," he said. "Bring Rainboy over and I'll give you a stall and a place to bed down." He let his car in gear, but before he could start, Big Red took the corral fence in a bound and trotted over to his feed rack. Carroll stared at the big horse calmly munching hay.

"That the clown Ranger?" He asked Leif. "Maybe you're training the wrong horse?"

Leif grinned and shook his head. His heart still pounded with the chance Carroll had given him. It would give Rainboy track experience, and Leif some idea of what Rainboy could do.

"Big Red's just a good-natured guy, Mr. Carroll," he explained. "Like's to bum around the road allowances and go swimming with the boys. But he's no runner."

"Well, so long, Leif. You should know," Jim Carroll drove his car slowly forward. "Be seeing you two days from now. McCarty'll have a fit you horning into this race. But that's okay—be seeing you."

With a wave to Big Chris getting stiffly out of his blue coupe, Carroll picked his way out of the machine-jammed yard and drove south toward his ranch.

Leif walked through the corral, past Big Red, who turned and gave him a slow stare, then on into the stall with Rainboy.

"Did you hear what went on, guy?" He asked, softly. "You're going to run against the colts you'll meet next year in the Stockman's."

Rainboy went on munching hay, standing straight on all four dainty hoofs.

"I heard it," Soren said, coming through the door. "I heard something else, too." He shook his head, slowly.

"Waite's saying all around he's got a claim on one of your colts—the best one."

Leif stared at Soren.

"But, we cancelled his note for what he owed us, and got Rebellious for it."

Soren's eyes squinted up at Leif's.

"Did you get anything in writing to prove it?"

"Big Chris was there," he said. Seeing Big Chris out beside an unsold binder, Leif had a notion to go out and talk it over right then. But, on second thought he didn't. Big Chris was almost distracted about his own troubles—no rain, no machinery selling and Culp waiting to grab the agency.

"Yeah, Big Chris—" Soren threw up his hands. "He's soft. Softer'n you are. You've got no chance against Waite."

Leif hid his concern behind a grin. He was still in the clouds about Carroll's offer. And this horse—Rainboy. He ran a hand down a sleek hind leg.

"We'll make out," he said. "Won't we, boy?"

Rainboy deigned no response. Just went on munching hay.

Two days later, as Leif drove his car and the trailer into Jim Carroll's yard, it looked as though he might be right that everything was going to be great.

Carroll, big and bluff, his voice echoing against the hills surrounding the spacious house and corrals of his ranch, met Leif in front of the big blue barn.

"Hi, Leif," he hailed. "Unload, and put him in here."

Leif's heart bounded with excitement.

"Okay, Mr. Carroll," he said. With a bound he was out of his car and in seconds had let down the tail gate to the trailer. "Easy, Rainboy," he soothed, leading the slim bay colt down the incline.

Off to the left of the barn, he caught sight of the race track. He wished he felt more sure of himself.

Rainboy stepped haughtily down the ramp of the trailer and on into the white-washed box stall. Clean gold wheat straw lay on the planked floor. Sweet green alfalfa stuck from the iron manger on one corner. Water, clear and sparkling, gurgled through a trough.

"Pretty swell, Rainboy," Leif whispered.

Rainboy acted as though he'd lived there always.

Suddenly, a horse from an adjoining stall whinnied sharply. His hoofs beat a rat-a-tat-tat on his box-stall door.

"Quiet, Combat," Carroll ordered. Then he turned to Leif. "Want to look over the colt that'll take Rainboy?"

"Let him come this way, then," a thin voice said. And it was McCarty. Still on the prod. Still the same tight-lipped bachelor. Leif wondered if there really was someone named Auntie McCarty who lived some place back in Vermont. Was there really a living being McCarty cared about?

Leif followed Carroll, with McCarty reluctantly drawing up the rear, over to see Combat Third.

Whitey Baker, slim, straw-colored as to hair and eyelashes, brought him out into the runway.

Leif felt something grip his insides. Could Rainboy beat this brown demon? He was a full hand taller than Rainboy, and rangy—

He felt the same sensation on down the barn, staring at the sorrel Pee Wee Parker held.

"Thunderbolt, out of Firebrand," McCarty snapped. "Gentlemen, take a look at the colt that'll take your two colts tomorrow, and the Stockman's next fall."

Carroll snorted.

Leif, still nervous, still speechless, followed the two men quietly back to the barn door.

The next afternoon he rode Rainboy down to the starting line. The track, a half-mile graded oval, was set in a meadow below the ranch house. Off to the west, the Rockies loomed tall and snow-capped.

"Twice around the track, Leif," Carroll boomed, his eyes going to his own colt, Combat Third, prancing toward the starting line.

"If he can make it," McCarty snapped. It was plain he thought his own sorrel, Thunderbolt, would win.

Leif nodded, and holding a tight rein on Rainboy, walked him abreast of the other two.

The dust of an approaching car formed a ribbon of brown haze on the skyline. Leif barely saw it. He could only see the track and know that here was Rainboy's first real test.

The horses stopped at the barrier—a thin tape stretched across the track.

Thunderbolt reared and fought Pee Wee's hold on his bit.

His unruliness spread to Combat, the big brown. He backed and kicked sharply at the air, then bolted forward.

Rainboy just stood staring coolly down the track.

"Old hand at this, you'd think," Carroll boomed, his hand on the starter spring that would send the tape up and the colts away—

Leif nodded. He was proud of Rainboy, but he didn't like the covetous look McCarty gave the horse. And here came sly Waite in his old crate. Getting out, after he'd screeched to a halt, he walked importantly over to McCarty.

Soren's warning flashed into Leif's mind. But it was only a flash. For Combat and Thunderbolt, worked to a lather, finally smoothed out to face the tape.

Jim Carroll's finger pressed the button. The tape sprang up and the three horses were off—

It was strictly a two-horse race from the start.

McCarty's Thunderbolt lagged all the way. Rainboy streaked to the turn, stretched out with Combat at his heels for the next quarter, then came flying past Carroll and McCarty.

"Come on, Combat!" Carroll boomed as they swept past.

McCarty, eying Thunderbolt a full three lengths back, clamped his thin lips a little tighter.

Leif stretched out over Rainboy's flying mane, and whispered in his ear, "Now, boy— Another lap. Come on—"

And Rainboy came on.

Combat pulled even in the backstretch. Hung on his nose through the final turn and into the stretch.

Leif loosened Rainboy's reins slightly.

"Now," he whispered to the sleek bay colt.

"Come on, Combat!" Carroll's voice reached down the track.

Leif shook the little horse's reins, felt the muscled back of Rainboy stretch out. Felt that last final "give," as he carried over the line a winner.

"By a nose," Carroll exclaimed, as Leif brought the blown colt back to the circle of men. "Boy, what a horse. I'd like to own him—"

"Maybe I'll sell him," a voice drawled. "If the price is right."

CHAPTER 7

Big Red's Heritage

FOR A MOMENT, Leif couldn't believe Waite would do anything so ornery as to grab Rainboy. He didn't own him.

"Sell him?" Leif repeated automatically as he began unsaddling the colt.

"If there's any buying, I'll do it," McCarty snapped.

Leif took hold of Rainboy's mane. His eyes went from one to the other. To Waite, standing with that slow grin sure on his long face. To McCarty, disgusted with Thunderbolt who'd been so badly whipped. It was evident that he wanted to buy a winner.

Suddenly Carroll said firmly, "Let's get this thing straight." He faced Leif and his voice gently asked, "Don't you own Rainboy, Leif? I thought—"

"That's just it," Waite drawled to Carroll. "There was too much thinking and not enough writing." He turned to Leif. "You got any paper to show you own Rainboy? Or for that matter that you owned his mother, Rebellious?"

"I happen to know that he hasn't," snapped McCarty, ignoring Leif and turning eagerly to Waite. "I'll give you five hundred dollars for him right now—five hundred dollars for Rainboy."

Leif had to protest, even though his sinking heart told him that Waite was right.

"But, for the note Big Chris and I cancelled, you gave us Rebellious," Leif protested to Waite.

"I didn't give you nothin'," Waite snapped. "You cancelled the note, then just took Rebellious. I was helpless. Helpless, I tell you."

"Get off my place, Waite," Carroll boomed, taking a step toward the grinning trader. "I didn't invite Leif down here to be insulted and robbed."

"Just a minute, Carroll," McCarty stepped in. "Have you got a bill of sale for the mother of this colt, Leif?"

Leif knew that he hadn't. He knew, too, the shrewd McCarty scented a chance to get a colt that would take the Stockman's from Carroll next fall. Slowly, Leif shook his head.

"It was a gentleman's agreement," he said.

McCarty ignored that, smiling thinly.

"Then, Waite," he turned to the slack form of the farmer beside him. "I'll give you the five hundred for Rainboy right now."

"I'll help you fight it in the courts," Carroll rolled out,

turning to Leif. "You've got witnesses—yourself and Big Chris."

Leif took his time. He stared from Carroll's honest face to Waite's plainly wanting the money. Then on to the dangerous one of McCarty. Suddenly, he knew that he was licked. McCarty was one of his father's best customers. He farmed a thousand acres of land. He bought a lot of haying machinery—was dickering for some right now. If Big Chris lost this sale and McCarty's account, then, Big Chris had lost the agency to Mr. Culp.

"No, Mr. Carroll," he said, gently stroking the silken foretop of Rainboy. "It was only a deal between friends. Legally, Rainboy belongs to Mr. Waite."

"And that other big red clown colt, too," Waite sneered. "But it looks like this one suits me right now."

Leif swallowed words that rushed to his lips. He turned to McCarty who looked plenty touchy.

"It's okay—Rainboy is Waite's to sell you."

McCarty nodded.

"I'm only buying what's legal," he said dryly. "What Big Chris, if he had any business sense, would have seen that you owned."

Leif suddenly felt the blood rush up his neck. Something boiling up within him, clenched his hands. He turned to McCarty and with astonishment heard his voice snap, "Big Chris has his own way of doing business. And

I'll get a horse that'll beat the socks off that colt you just bought, Mr. McCarty. Beat the socks off him, see?"

"Humph!" snapped McCarty. "When I get through training that colt, nothing'll beat him."

Leif turned and, gathering up his saddle, walked toward Carroll's barn. He felt foolish and windy. For where was there a colt he could get that would beat Rainboy?

Carroll caught up with him and walked alongside.

"A fine way to entertain a friend," he said. "Sorry, Leif. And anything I can do—" His voice sounded hopeless, too.

Leif nodded. His eyes stung, and there was a gone feeling in the pit of his stomach. Boy, had he made a fool of himself before a lot of men!

"Thanks, Mr. Carroll," he said. "And thank Mrs. Carroll for me, too."

He loaded his stuff quickly into his car and, with the empty trailer clattering behind, drove the outfit down the trail to the highway, then took the gravel road into Magrath.

It was dusk as he hit the gravel. In half an hour it would be dark. He passed McCarty's low ranch buildings within twenty minutes—the low ranch barns, the one-story white house in which McCarty lived alone. Off to the left of them lay the meadows where McCarty's herd of thoroughbred mares usually ran.

"Hey!" Leif pulled his car to a halt and stared at a hole in the five-foot woven fence. "A hole!" he breathed. His eyes searched the mile-square lot. "And no mares. They must be on the loose." He paused a moment, then started his car once more. He'd call McCarty the moment he got home.

He drove on, his mind racing through the possibilities of getting another colt, and always coming to a dead-end stop. There wasn't much time. Just this winter and until next Fair Day—probably some day late in August.

Suddenly, it was almost dark. He could scarcely see the road gliding under his front wheels. Leif switched on the lights, staring a mile and a half ahead, at the answering ones of Magrath.

He sure hated to face Soren, and Big Chris who'd been watching him with Rainboy. Probably knowing what Leif had up his sleeve, but not saying much.

Suddenly, a quarter of a mile farther along the road, Leif all but ran into a herd of mares. McCarty's mares. He could see their sleek sides, their slim legs, the predominance of sorrels. The blood-strain of Firebrand, McCarty's sorrel stallion.

Leif slackened his car, then stared, as a big colt separated himself from the mares, with a snort and an arched neck.

Leif grinned wispily.

The big clown, he thought, watching Big Red. For it was Big Red, tail erect, head high, and stepping out in front of the car. "You want to race, eh?"

Big Red snorted once more. He whinnied and pranced along. Almost daring Leif to run him down.

Leif, his mind still filled with Rainboy, gently pressed the throttle down.

"Okay, Big Red," he called. "Let's go!" It sort of eased him.

The car crept up toward the big running shape—right on that plume of black tail that crept away, as the big colt's powerful legs lengthened their stride.

Leif gave the car more gas. The car slid through the dark. That speedometer said plenty miles per hour.

Still the big red colt stretched ahead.

Leif pressed the throttle harder, his eyes on the speedometer, but his mind on Rainboy.

A quarter of a mile flashed past, a half, three quarters. And then, the mile. And there was Magrath, with Big Red whipping to the side of the roadside and, with a flourish of his heels, racing back toward his mares.

His mind still on the colt he'd lost, Leif let his eyes measure the full mile, and the speed, then without more thought, drove on into the yard. Mercifully, Soren was down at Swanson's, visiting with the storekeeper.

Leif put up the car and trailer, then walked into the

house and washed his face and hands at the kitchen washstand. Drying, absentmindedly on a roller towel, he sat down at one side of the big oak kitchen table.

"Big Chris won't be back tonight," Anna said, with a quick glance at Leif's sober face. Setting baked ham, potatoes, fried golden brown, and beets round and red, before him, she added, "He's gone with Turner to Lethbridge."

Leif dully filled his plate with food and mechanically began to eat. He knew what that meant. They were raking Big Chris over the coals about all the machinery he'd sold on notes. And asking him how, with the drouth, he expected to get it back.

Looking out of the kitchen window at the starlit sky, Leif heard the soft sigh of a dry wind. The same dry wind that had blown all summer. That had dried up the crops completely.

Finishing supper, he crept up the stairs and into the room he and Big Chris had slept in ever since his mother had died. Sitting on the side of the bed, he racked his brains. Where, oh, where was he going to get a colt—a fast colt?

One shoe hit the floor. And another. His clothes slipped off his aching body. He slid into his blue pyjamas and crawled under the big brown comforter—it was the last thing Mother had made. He pulled it up over his slim shoulders and lay staring out the window.

A million stars. A million. Guess they must be going plenty fast— He yawned. Plenty fast all right. Like Big Red, shooting down that road at over forty miles an hour. Leif yawned again and, dozing, suddenly let his mind figure out how fast Big Red had run. Suddenly, he sat bolt up right. His heart was beating so hard he could hardly hear it.

"Big Red, you big clown," he whispered, getting into his clothes. "You beat Rainboy's time for that mile. You're that colt I've been looking for." He ran downstairs and out into the starlit night. Yet Leif was afraid to believe Big Red was that good.

"Where are you going, Leif?" Anna called from her little bedroom window.

"To get Big Red back in his corral," he said cautiously.

He backed the car out, turned it up the road and ran swiftly back along the way he'd come.

Big Red wasn't in sight. Nor the mares.

Leif ran three miles, then doubled back.

Still no colt.

Leif pulled his car to a halt, a feeling of dread mounting within him. "Gone—swallowed up!" he whispered.

Suddenly, off to the left and into the expanse that led up toward Grizzly Pass, he heard the high shrill neigh of a horse.

Leif puzzled. It didn't sound like Big Red. And yet, it did. And then, suddenly, Leif knew. Big Red had grown up. He had become, overnight, a full-grown stallion with a band of mares.

"And," Leif whispered, thinking of McCarty, thinking of that vast expanse of land that Big Red could hide his band in, "I've lost him."

Slowly, he drove back to his yard and put the car back in the garage.

Walking toward the house, he knew he'd have to call McCarty in the morning and tell him the truth about Big Red and the mares. McCarty, being McCarty, would blow his top. There'd be trouble.

CHAPTER 8

McCarty Vows Vengeance

IN THE MORNING, Leif was just as sure of trouble. He got out of bed before daylight. Ahead of McCarty's trouble, he thought. He'd get his car and cruise out the highway, maybe pick up Big Red and the mares before McCarty could know they were gone.

But driving out along the road allowances, he got no trace of Big Red. Neither the big horse, nor the mares, were in sight.

The east grew light.

Leif gulped. McCarty would be getting up about now. With a leaden feeling at the pit of his empty stomach, Leif swung the pickup truck to the right and off across the prairie. He drove for twenty miles, then stopped the car on Lookout Hill.

Getting stiffly to the grass, he walked the hundred feet to the edge.

Sweet Grass Run lay before him—a hundred square miles of worthless government grazing land. Land unfamiliar to him, but to McCarty, born and raised right here, an open book.

Leif let his blue eyes run along its hilly surface. A groan escaped him. Somewhere out there, in one of the swales, grazed Big Red, the horse he must get back. He opened his mouth and whistled the low coaxing note his horses knew.

Nothing came back—not even an echo in the early morning light.

Leif felt a foolish smile spread across his face. He was suddenly, a little scared.

McCarty would comb these hills. Ten thoroughbred mares, worth three thousand dollars, he wouldn't pass up without a struggle. He'd track Big Red down. Outwit him. Maybe trail him till he'd get close enough to drop him with a bullet behind the ear, making the mares an easy capture.

Leif, keeping his eyes averted from Grizzly Pass, walked back to his car and started the engine. He wouldn't admit, even to himself, what would happen to Big Red if he foolishly should drift up into the mountains.

He pictured McCarty's dry laugh of glee, then.

For there, McCarty could get him—corner him on the narrow cliff edge of Waterton Lake, and either shoot him or let the big red horse dive to his death in the lake.

Leif let in his clutch and, turning the car around, headed for home.

Driving along, Leif couldn't bring himself to face McCarty yet. Let the man cool off, or maybe he'd still find Big Red. Some miracle might happen— He swung the car around and headed deep into Sweet Grass Run. Along level stretches of prairie, down coulees, over little creeks, Leif guided the car. Herds of white-faced cattle met his gaze, but no big red horse circling a band of sorrel mares. No young stallion, stepping proudly in the first flush of maturity.

A band of scrub horses—a black scrub stallion at their head—topped the crest of a hill.

Leif, watching how quickly they'd come into sight, and how fast they disappeared down a gully, kicking and rearing, turned sick. In five minutes, though they were less than a mile from him, they might as well have been in another world.

He guided his car to the right and drove it hard up the trail leading to the mountains. Some inner feeling, some idea that later, with Big Red trapped and McCarty and his riders closing in, he might save Big Red's life if he knew the terrain drove Leif on. He left the car under a big spruce tree at the end of the trail and hiked the three miles to come out on the cliffs overlooking Waterton Lake.

Leif paid no attention to the beauty of the long oval lake, nor to the wooded mysterious island lying directly across the lake and close to the opposite shore.

"Cliffs," he whispered, staring down beyond his feet. An icy hand, colder than the deep blue water of the lake, clutched him. "Cliffs that no horse could pick a way down, nor jump from and live."

Leif stood mute and silent, driven by some inner presentiment. His eyes took in every detail of the cliffs on both sides of him, ranged across the lake to Lost Island, then beyond to swerve left and up the trail to Grizzly Pass. It was the only way back, once Lost Island was gained.

Suddenly, his mind filled with the scene, Leif turned and made his way back to his car. More than ever he wanted to keep away from McCarty, now. There must be some way to keep him from starting his merciless tracking down of Big Red.

Leif waited till dusk, then drove back to the highway and, on impulse, to the right and by McCarty's ranch. He'd just buzz by, fast. Maybe the mares had drifted back—and Big Red with them—

But the paddock was empty, with the fence repaired. The low white ranch house had a grim deserted look.

Getting up his courage, Leif risked going into the lane leading to the big red McCarty barn. Pulling up before the door, he knew why the place had looked deserted.

"The boss is lookin' for you, kid," Pee Wee said from the barn doorway. He had Rainboy tied between two rings and was sponging his sleek bay body with water in a big brown sponge. "An' is he burned!"

Leif got out of his pickup truck and walked over to Rainboy.

"Why?" he asked softly, grinning, yet feeling the uselessness of pretending. "What've I done?"

"Not you, that big red clown of yours—he's run off with McCarty's herd of racing mares."

Leif waited till he could speak easily. He pulled at Rainboy's combed mane, hoping Rainboy would show some sign of recognition.

"How's he know that?" he asked.

Rainboy impatiently shook his head, thrusting Leif away.

Pee Wee snickered.

"Say, McCarty wasn't born yesterday—with that red tramp colt roaming the road allowances. Then this morning he ain't around, nor the mares, either. Get smart, kid."

Dully Leif watched Pee Wee grooming Rainboy. The colt stood soaking it up like a spoiled brat.

"I don't know why McCarty should jump to the conclusion Big Red swiped his mares," he objected.

Pee Wee turned toward Leif, the dripping sponge in his clawlike hand.

"Well, he did." He grinned from a shrivelled face. "And boy, did McCarty fork his bronc and light out—him and his riders. I wouldn't want to be Big Red."

"Which way did they go?" Leif asked, knowing before he asked.

"Guess?" Pee Wee snorted, snapping Rainboy's rope loose and leading the mincing colt into his boxstall.

Leif turned to go, climbing doggedly behind the wheel. Pee Wee came back to stand by his car.

"Why don't you let McCarty track the clown down and shoot him? He's no good, anyway."

Leif knew there was no use in arguing with Pee Wee. He felt a desperate need to keep away from McCarty to-night. Maybe by morning the mares would straggle home. Big Red was just short of three years old and not skilled in herding a band as yet.

He turned the car over, let in the gears and drove out to the highway, then turned toward Jim Carroll's. Maybe Jim would have an idea? But as he drove into the Carroll yard and up to the big two-story white house, he sensed that his quest was useless.

Ah Sing, the cook, came to the door, grinning from ear to ear.

"Missy Carroll's gone by Lethbridge—be home three days," he chattered. "Me helpy you—"

Leif smiled sadly. There was something pretty funny in Ah Sing offering to help—to catch Big Red?

"No, guess not, Ah Sing," he said, and once more headed the car toward the highway.

It had been a full day by the time Leif drove into his own yard. For a moment, pulling up just outside the corral, he got a shock. For over the fence top a horse's head loomed.

"Big Red," he whispered, jumping from the car and walking swiftly toward the corral gate.

"Yeah?" McCarty's dry scornful laugh came from beside the horse—his saddle horse and not Big Red.

"You think he won't come back?" Leif asked, facing him there.

McCarty's thin face grew bleak and bitter.

"No—he won't," he snapped. "My men'll probably shoot him. Listen—here they come now. They've probably shot him and are bringing my mares."

Leif gulped and stood silent. It could be true. Big Red would probably march right up to McCarty's riders, the big dope.

Above the pounding hoofs of approaching horses a voice called, "Leif! Leif!" It was Anna. "You better come while supper's hot—no breakfast, you must be starved."

"In a minute, Anna," Leif called back. The horses were dark shapes in the night. He had to see if Big Red was among them.

But McCarty's inarticulate cry of rage when six riders,

hazing no mares before them, came through the gate, told Leif that, for the moment at any rate, Big Red was safe.

He bent then to doing what he'd wanted to do all along. First by staying clear of McCarty, and now by persuasion.

"Let's give Big Red a day or two to bring the mares back," he said softly to McCarty.

McCarty swung to him.

"Shut up!" Then he turned to Smiley Brand. "Well?"

Smiley, short and chubby, with a sunny face and blue eyes, swung to the ground, shrugging round plump shoulders.

"Not a hair, boss." He grinned. "We been ridin' since daylight—covered half of Sweet Grass Run—" He shrugged again, to show how futile their search for the big red horse had been.

McCarty snorted in disgust.

Leif tried again.

"Your mares'll be safe with Big Red," he reminded.

McCarty's burning eyes made Leif recoil.

"And next summer, I'll get a crop of scrub colts," he barked.

"He's got the same blood lines as Rainboy, Leif retorted. "You paid five hundred dollars for him."

"He's a scrub—a big red scrub," McCarty snapped. "I'm going to—"

Leif didn't want McCarty to say, "I'll kill him!" Even though it was range law.

"Listen, Mr. McCarty," he put in hastily. "I'll tell you something—a secret about Big Red." Quietly, he told him about the colt's race with the car, and the time he'd made for the mile.

When he'd finished, McCarty didn't move a muscle.

A dog howled in the distance. A lonesome howl that sank Leif's heart to zero.

"So," Leif finally said, for he could see it was the only way to save Big Red's life, "if you'll promise to take him alive, you can have him."

Still McCarty made no sign.

Leif made a last try.

"Big Red's going to be faster than Rainboy," he pleaded. "A lot faster—and he's yours if you'll let him live."

McCarty made no reply.

A coyote, off on the ridge, answered the dog. Anna's pans rattled from the kitchen. Leif could hardly breathe.

Suddenly, McCarty swung to Smiley Brand, ignoring Leif completely.

"Git on home with your men," he snarled. "To-morrow, I'll head the hunting party. We'll knock that big red scrub off quick and bring in my mares."

He swung into his saddle and started out the corral gate.

They'd be up at daylight. With McCarty knowing
Sweet Grass Run as he did— Leif's eyes flew to an empty
saddle on an extra horse Smiley held.

"Mr. McCarty!" His voice sounded high and tinny.

McCarty reined in his sorrel and looked sharply over
his thin high shoulder. "Well?"

"I, I guess you're right about Big Red," Leif stam-
mered. "But if you're going to hunt him, do you mind if
I ride that extra horse and go along?"

McCarty sat immovable, figuring.

Leif could scarcely breathe, waiting for his answer.
For he had a plan to save Big Red and give McCarty
back his mares. If he could only go along—

Then McCarty nodded and snapped to Smiley, "Give
him the horse."

Leif, his heart bounding, climbed silently into the
saddle and followed the riders filing out the yard toward
the street. Seeing Anna at the kitchen door, he reined
over to her to leave a message for Big Chris.

"You eat?" Anna asked, her blue eyes big and anxious.

"At McCarty's—and tell Big Chris I'm going to ride
with McCarty and his men tomorrow. I've got to find
Big Red."

He rode after the retreating men. At the yard gate
Soren stopped him, hanging at his left stirrup, his pudgy
hands trembling with concern.

"You crazy?" He shook Leif's leg. "I heard it all.

You're not going to see Big Red shot. You've got some crazy scheme that won't work—"

"Just keep the Agency till Big Chris comes, to-morrow," Leif said. "That's all." With a prod of his feet, he started the horse under him down the road to overtake McCarty and his riders. Maybe his scheme was crazy, but he had to try it. He urged the horse to a gallop and rode on.

CHAPTER 9

Leif's Desperate Ruse

LEIF WOKE the next morning to the sound of the north wind howling around the corner of the McCarty bunkhouse. His first paralyzing thought was that on this day Big Red might get shot.

"Snow!" Smiley grinned, leaping to the pine-board floor and pulling on his levis. "Brr! I sure hate the idea of riding herd on that big red clown and his band today."

"Yeah." Texas Perkins, a tall gangling puncher, rolled over and cocked an eye at Smiley. "Why can't we just go on sleepin'?"

Leif, sleepily pulling on his cords, nodded. He avoided looking at Smiley, or the other punchers. His plan admitted of no one riding Sweet Grass Run but McCarty and himself. He pulled on his sweater and leather jumper, then ducking his head against the sharp north wind made it to the barn.

He hoped McCarty wouldn't be there. He wanted him full of breakfast and hot coffee before he suggested that they ride alone—bring in the band together.

94

McCarty wasn't there. But his orders, written out in that small precise handwriting on red-lined paper, were.

"Well, lad," Smiley, who'd come in, said. "We've got it to do." He looked at the small sheet of paper he'd picked up at McCarty's ranch house on the way to the barn.

Leif's heart squeezed shut, as he watched Smiley brush down his roan gelding and toss his big tooled-leather saddle aboard.

"Sweet Grass Run—Big Red—" he gulped. "McCarty hasn't changed his mind?"

"Nope!" Smiley nodded. "The boss doesn't want his mares to spend the winter on Sweet Grass Run."

Leif numbly saddled his horse—watching Smiley finish his own, then go on to McCarty's private riding horse. It was the same big blaze-faced sorrel he'd ridden last night.

Leif couldn't keep his eyes off that Winchester 30-30 in its scabbard strapped to the saddle.

"Does McCarty always carry that gun?" he asked softly. He waited a long time for the reply.

Then Smiley's red round face showed sympathy for him.

"Wears it like his pants." He nodded. "Maybe tighter," he added.

Punchers around Leif laughed at Smiley. Even Pee

Wee down the barn runway where the box stalls were, laughed thinly.

Leif finished his horse and walked close to Smiley.

"You've known McCarty a long time, Smiley," he said. "What do you think he likes best in all the world?"

"That's easy," Smiley slapped the sorrel on the rump and walked out to Leif. "Some female back in Vermont named 'Auntie.' Next to fast-racing horses. The faster the better."

Leif felt his heart jump against his ribs.

"Then maybe," he said, softly, "maybe if I could just get him and me to go. And I could station him on a hill and haze Big Red by—fast—McCarty'd see Big Red as he really is. Maybe he'd even forget to shoot, and—"

Smiley shook his head. "I guess I forgot to tell you. There's one thing McCarty likes better than either of those things I told you and that's not to change his opinion. He's got hates on his mind that've worn right down into his sharp brain. And he's proud of 'em."

Leif studied Smiley's eyes, but he stubbornly refused to believe the puncher's words.

"You're wrong, Smiley," he said, turning to go with him toward the sound of the cook-house gong. "McCarty'll watch Big Red sail past. He'll have a chance to shoot, but he'll drop his gun and just stare. The next minute he'll want Big Red worse than anything he ever wanted."

Smiley just gave Leif a thin grin and pushed on toward the cook house off to the left of the bunkhouse.

Leif clung to this opinion. It helped him when he faced McCarty after breakfast, with the north wind making smoke come out of their mouths and McCarty's eyes as icy as the snow clouds scudding past.

"Well, boys," McCarty stood just outside the cook house with the six punchers ringed around him. "Ready?"

Leif took a deep breath, then with his heart hammering, spat out, "Yeah, boys—all six of you and the boss to bring in ten mares."

McCarty grunted as from a blow and swung to face Leif.

Being ornery came hard to Leif. He laughed harshly—not a bad imitation of McCarty's own.

"If this gets to Carroll's riders they'll laugh you so-called punchers out of Alberta." He let his eyes go mockingly around the group, then met McCarty's square.

"Jim Carroll will get quite a bang of you too, Mr. McCarty," he said, softly. "Headin' such a posse."

McCarty's eyes pin-pointed on Leif.

And suddenly Leif saw that he'd dented McCarty's defense.

"How about us doing this alone, Mr. McCarty?" He thrust in "It's about our size. Or maybe"—he stifled a grin—"maybe you'd like to send Smiley? It's going to snow and you're not so young—"

His words were cut off by McCarty's rasping order, "Smiley, take the boys and ride that east fence. Bring in those yearlings and start workin' them over for the halter. If you get that done—"

But Leif didn't hear any more. He walked rapidly down to the barn to wait for McCarty.

"You're a sap," Pee Wee sidled in to sneer. "McCarty's a dead shot—you've as good as killed your own scrub colt."

Leif shut his ears to Pee Wee. McCarty was a horse lover. When he saw Big Red coming up wind, head stretched out, legs pounding, and that big red body flashing past, there'd be nothing to it.

"Let me handle that," he said, softly. "You just get that sissy Rainboy ready for the licking Big Red's going to hand him at the Fair next fall."

Pee Wee didn't move, beyond shifting his wiry frame from his left foot to his right.

"You're crazy," he said. "That big red bozo'll get popped off today—he'll probably walk right into McCarty's gun-barrel."

Leif had thought of that. He gulped, then shook his head.

"Big Red's got his band," he said, stoutly. "He'll shy clear of any gunman."

Pee Wee shrugged and lowered his voice for McCarty's quick step sounded just outside the barn.

"Remember, you asked for it," He said. "And remember, too. Nothing works out like you plan it."

Leif didn't bother to nod. This thing would. He turned to untie his brown gelding and pull him out of the stall, bridle him, then get on.

"Here!" Smiley, who'd come in with McCarty, tossed him a sheep-lined coat. "Put this on, lad."

Leif, not knowing that Smiley by this act had saved his life, caught the coat, shrugged it on, then followed McCarty's big sorrel out the gate and toward the rolling foothills.

Clouds, low and filled with snow, scudded by. Particles stung Leif's face as they rode wordlessly along.

It was high noon and clear by the time they reached Lookout Point. The clouds, with only a black bank to the north, had broken, making visibility good.

"Boy!" Leif told himself. "Big Red's coat'll sure glisten in this sun." He glanced at McCarty, who snapped, "We'll spread out. Ride every gully, Leif. And if you flush him, just sneak back and tell me."

Leif nodded soberly, but felt his heart go light. If he flushed Big Red, there was just one thing to do: haze him past McCarty and let that big red body glistening in the sun do the rest.

Leif reined his horse to the right and rode off at an

angle to McCarty. After a quarter of a mile, he reined
his horse once more and rode parallel to McCarty, keeping a sharp lookout for horses.

They rode for an hour. Two hours.

Once, Leif sighted a band of eleven ahead.

McCarty'd seen them, too, and waved Leif forward.
Closing in.

Leif found his breath coming short, and his heart
thudding. A dry taste came to his mouth.

But suddenly, coming closer, Leif felt relief flood him.
The band wasn't Big Red and his mares, but only an
Indian band headed by a brown cayuse horse. Kicking,
biting at each other's necks, they disappeared down a
draw. Lost to sight in a moment.

"Humph!" McCarty snapped. "I thought we'd flushed
that red thief."

Leif, warm with relief, did not answer, beyond a careful nod.

They rode on.

Around noon, Leif heard a shot. He stared off toward
McCarty. No one was in sight. Numbly, his hands
turned his brown gelding. With his heart in his mouth
he raced over the hill. And there was the tough McCarty
sitting his horse and staring off to the hill beyond.

"Just a young wolf stalking a colt," he snapped,
testily, and re-holstering his gun. "Let's get along."

Leif felt like tossing his hat into the sunny air.

"Ashamed of showing how much he wanted to protect an innocent sucking colt," Leif whispered. Suddenly, he felt more sure than ever that McCarty wouldn't shoot Big Red.

The two riders fanned out again, and the old hunt took up again.

They rode till two o'clock—three. Till McCarty, pulling over to Leif as they sat a ridge, said, shortly, "Guess we'll have to give it up for today."

Leif recognized relief in McCarty's tones. So the man had had time to think it over? And by tomorrow, he'd be reasonable about Big Red.

"Yeah," Leif agreed. He felt that now Big Red would have the winter with the mares. Pawing snow from the ground for food. Fighting off wolves and herding the mares against encroaching horses. Keeping the McCarty blood lines clear. "Yeah, let's go," he added.

But the words faded from his lips. His eyes bulged from their sockets. For less than half a mile distant and straight ahead, coming up a coulee, walked Big Red himself. Behind him trotted McCarty's precious mares.

The big horse tossed his head. He danced playfully toward them.

Leif heard McCarty draw a sharp breath. All that softness had gone out of him, seeing Big Red with his mares.

"Drop behind this hill," he whispered sharply to Leif. "Once I shoot that scrub stud, the mares'll be easy to take home."

"Why not take them all?" Leif whispered back.

"And let that big bozo lead them away?" McCarty's eyes glinted on Leif's.

The two riders dropped behind the hill. Leif circled along the draw and came up behind the band.

"Git going, Big Red," he whooped.

The big horse tossed his head, reared toward Leif, then faced toward McCarty.

Leif followed, watching the mares and stallion race on. Suddenly, he reined in. The band would go past McCarty of their own momentum now.

He swung around, dully waiting for the crack of McCarty's gun; hearing the fading beat of the horses.

But no gunshot came. Nothing but the distant pound of hoofs that must be well past McCarty by now. Leif reined his horse around and rode toward McCarty, a question in his mind: why hadn't McCarty shot? Then, following McCarty riding straight for his ranch, Leif knew. McCarty'd seen Big Red as Leif saw him. He hadn't been able to shoot him. He didn't want Leif to see what a weak fool he'd been.

Leif grinned and, leaning down, patted his horse's sweaty neck. Following McCarty at a distance, and riding rather carelessly, Leif rode too close to a cut-bank.

The horse fought against the caving bank, then went over and down a full ten feet.

Leif went with him.

Horse and rider fell free of each other and scrambled to their feet.

The next instant, the saddle horse made for a short-cut way to the home ranch. And Leif, running vainly after him, felt the first flurries of snow. In ten minutes, still running, Leif knew he was in for it. It was getting dark, and a blizzard engulfed him.

CHAPTER 10

The Red Shadow

LEIF'S FIRST IMPULSE running against the swirling snow was to shout for help. He had a flash of Big Chris, lonesome and running that failing business alone.

"Father! Father!" he shouted.

The racing wind took the words from his lips so fast he barely heard them himself.

Leif increased his speed, sure that he was heading toward Magrath and Big Chris. There was work for him to do. He brought up sharply at tracks—his own tracks, now half covered with skidding icy streams of drifting snow.

"Running in a circle," he gasped.

Panting, he started again, doggedly this time, and veering off to the left, keeping always to the left. This time he'd make it. He'd get home to be alive in the spring. To capture Big Red and train him for the Stockman's.

For an hour, he walked, then suddenly stopped.

Darkness folded a wet black wall around him. Leif held out his numb hand and couldn't see it. He whistled in amazement. And again that icy feeling of panic seized him.

A herd of cattle, heads down, their backs snow laden, passed so close he could touch the crumpled right horn of the lead range cow. Leif knew that they'd find shelter under some cut-bank, and huddle together till the storm broke, one, two, or even three days hence.

He walked with them, but their sharp horns, hooking as they drifted, filled him with concern. One lunge, one blow of a horn against him by a cow thinking he was only another, and he'd be down for good. The snow'd drift over him. He'd not be found till spring.

He veered off from them, trying to follow from a distance.

They faded into the pitch black. Voiceless as they were, they seemed woolly spirits shrieking. "But of course that was only the wind. The cattle were silent and only drifting," he told himself, with a wry smile that cracked his numb snowy face.

Leif began searching for a gully. He could lie down in it. The snow would drift over him and he'd be warm and safe. But it seemed there were no gullies.

"Never saw such a flat country," he breathed. Suddenly, he started raging. He shook his fist in the snow filled air and bawled, "Not a coulee. Not a hole!"

Suddenly, his right foot sank, throwing him forward on his face. He struggled up, wiping the snow from his lips and there was a sticky smear on his glove.

"Blood—cut my lip," he said, back-tracking to find the hole. Hoping it would be the edge of a coulee.

It was a hole about a foot in diameter and running off at an angle.

"Be fine, if I was a badger," he muttered, with a grimace. He wandered on, fighting through the snow. It was hard walking now, and like going through fine white powder.

"Keep moving, Leif," he whispered. "Keep moving! Lie down and you'll go to sleep. And you know what that means—"

He plowed on. A sleepiness crept over him. He gritted his teeth and fought on. Flailing his arms against his cold body.

"Keep moving! Keep moving!"

For what seemed hours to Leif, he kept this up. Moving along, a snow-laden ball humped against the wind. First quickly, then gradually slowing. Picking up speed, then slowing—

At last, at the end of each spurt, he stopped. Knowing the danger, still he stopped. Even as he whispered "Keep moving, keep moving, Leif. For Big Chris's sake," he'd sink to the snow and close his eyes.

But each time, as he slumped there, with the snow starting that little mounding against his body, Leif roused and fought on.

But there came a time when he did not get up. That voice within him warned, "You'll freeze."

He felt the snow mound against him, and instead of filling him with panic, it lulled him.

"Bed—" he said. "Warm—"

He sagged to the ground and could not rise.

But something in the way he lay made a funnel for the wind. It whistled under his left arm. A long low whistle. The same sound as the one he'd used to call Big Red.

Leif smiled slightly.

"Big Red," he whispered. "Big Red!" He fixed his attention on it. And suddenly, he opened ice-crusted lips, pursed them in a round O and whistled.

The wind carried it from him.

He shook his head. But he whistled again, and again, and again.

No figure emerged from the snow. No big red shape came lunging out of the darkness to him.

Leif shook his head, and let it sag to his chest.

"Nice," he said. "Warm—"

He whistled once more—a low whistle with no steam behind it. Then he stretched out along the ground, his face buried between bent arms.

"Nice—" he said to himself. "Nice and warm—" A pleasing warmth stole over him. He dreamed he was in bed beside Big Chris. And Big Chris was saying: "Good night, Leif—" in that big warm voice of his.

Suddenly, a nicker sounded by Leif's left ear.

"Go 'way—" He stirred.

The nicker sounded again.

"Go 'way—" Leif threw out an arm. And let it fall back to cover his face. But then, a hoof pawed his shoulder.

With a mighty effort, Leif raised his head.

"Red shadow—" he breathed, staring through the dark. "Red shadow—"

The nicker came again. And the hoof pawing—

Leif brushed at his forehead, consciousness slowly returning. "Big Red," he finally said.

Big Red nickered, and dropped his head down against Leif's face.

Leif put out his hand to push it away. His fingers locked in Big Red's forelock, and with an effort he pulled himself to his feet.

Big Red's body was warm. Leif leaned against it. Blood started flowing through him again. He made a mighty effort and fought to climb on Big Red's back. The huge horse started moving off, as though he knew where he was headed.

WHEN Leif came to, the sun was shining. He tried to sit up and said, "Ouch!" Rubbing his head that had bumped on a ledge above him, his eyes turned toward the light and saw a lot of legs, horses' legs, as they stood banked against the ledge patiently waiting the storm's ebb.

"McCarty's mares," Leif said, crawling out. "And Big Red!"

The big horse stirred, shook himself free of snow as Leif edged along the herd to him.

"Big Red," Leif said, huskily. "You saved my life."

Big Red nickered softly, then turned his body sharply.

The whole band was rousing. Hunger gnawed at them, Leif could tell. They'd fan out onto the prairie, digging clumps of grass from under the vast white expanse before him.

Leif felt hunger too. It gripped his belly. He put a hand on Big Red's mane and sprang to his back.

"Red," he said. "You can stay with the band all winter. But first, you're taking me home." He moved the big horse up the draw and, sighting by the snow-covered Rockies off to the left, urged him toward Magrath.

For miles, Big Red and Leif fought through the snow, till suddenly, on a knoll ahead, loomed the searching party.

Leif rode toward them, till he was sure they'd sighted him, then slipped from Big Red's back and stood beside the steaming horse.

"Well, Big Red," he said, softly, pulling the horse's nose down to his face. "Be seeing you in the spring—and, thanks."

The great horse let his black nose rest a moment on Leif's cheek, then with a sudden whinny, wheeled and disappeared in a cloud of flying snow.

Leif turned and walked slowly toward the six men on horseback who were coming to meet him. That big blond giant whose horse was breaking track, Leif knew at once.

"Father," he whispered, increasing his speed. "And Smiley Brand with four other punchers—but no McCarty?"

A fear gripped him.

It was soon confirmed.

A hundred yards from Leif, Big Chris boomed out, "Hi, Leif!"

Even at that distance, Leif could see that big ruddy face glowing with happiness. But as the group came riding up, a silence settled over them.

"Seen anything of McCarty?" Smiley asked. "We hoped he'd be with you."

Leif scrambled up behind Big Chris, then shook his head. In a dozen words he told about Big Red. About McCarty's riding off. About his own horse's tumble, and his escape at the hoofs of Big Red.

Big Chris nodded, and grinned. He let out a whoop that startled a covey of prairie chickens from the snow.

Through the skimming whirr of their wings, came Smiley's voice.

"Well, he's lost."

The men exchanged glances.

Smiley went on, voicing all their thoughts, "We'll give finding him everything we've got. But if McCarty's fallen in a gully or an earthquake fault, it might be August before his body's recovered."

After a long silence, Big Chris nodded.

Silently, then, by common consent, they spread out and began a search for McCarty's slim hunched snow-hidden body.

For days they searched. Riding out each day from the ranch. But they didn't find him.

At last, they all rode home.

"In the spring," they said. "In the spring—"

Leif, too, riding with them, said, "In the spring—" They would find McCarty then. He was sorry the way it had turned out. He, too, had something to do in the spring—to capture Big Red and train him for the Stockman's Race. For Big Chris and somehow for McCarty, too, who had lost his life giving a horse a break.

He did not know about McCarty. But the man, knowing that he was in for it, that the snow would get him, had reached into his pocket for the will he always carried. With stiffening fingers he had written, *And to Leif Olson—*

CHAPTER II

Waite Strikes Again

B UT THE NEXT SPRING, that started out as dry as the year before, Leif wasn't alone in wanting to capture Big Red.

He was out in the machine yard setting up a drill when Waite rode in on a lean brown mare and pulled up less than five feet from him.

"I'm just warnin' you," Waite's drawl came as dry as the west wind. "I'm aimin' to catch Big Red myself—or run him off Waterton Cliff."

Leif picked up a drill disc and a crescent wrench, then looked Waite over. It was plain to see that he was still poverty-ridden — that he'd spent the five hundred McCarty had given him for Rainboy—that to capture Big Red he'd go to any length.

"Big Red is my horse and you know it."

Waite waved a scrawny hand, and his crafty eyes narrowed on Leif. "Where's your brand—you didn't get no mark on Big Red, did you?"

Leif, dropping to the grass to start shoving a disc on a drill that wouldn't sell, shook his head.

"Then, he's a maverick," Waite crowed. "And a maverick belongs to the first man who tosses a rope on him. Then irons him."

Leif didn't answer. He should have branded Big Red. But he never could get over trusting people. And then there was Big Chris—off to Lethbridge again. Summoned there by Turner, the block-man, a good friend of Chris', but still a businessman who wanted results, who had to have them, with the I.H.C. pressing for payments. And of course, back of all else loomed Mr. Culp. Always hovering around ready to grab the Agency.

"Well, so long, Leif." Waite swung his horse to go. "No hard feelin's I hope. An' if I get that big red clown and win the Stockman's, I'll give you a slice of what I sell him for."

Leif jumped to his feet and fixed steady blue eyes on Waite. He really felt sorry for this man—and it wasn't right to let him get away with this.

Waite tried to meet Leif's eyes, blinked, then let his eyes swing around the almost empty machine yard. To the shed that peeled under the blistering sun. To the house, silent, with the shades down. Anna had gone— there'd been no money to pay her wages.

"You're all but broke," Waite sneered. "I guess you could use anything I give you."

"Thanks, Waite," Leif said, softly. "But I'm getting Big Red and winning the Stockman's, myself."

Waite laughed dryly, and kicked his gaunt horse in the ribs as he rode out to meet his gang just outside the yard.

Leif dropped to the grass and went to work on the disc once more. A fever took possession of him. Just five weeks till the Stockman's Race. Five weeks to catch Big Red and get to Lethbridge.

Soren came from the red machine shed.

"That Waite'll do it, too," he burst out, as he stooped down to look at Leif. "He's uncanny."

Leif, twisting on a burr with the crescent, shook his head. The determination that had carried him through so many things, filled him.

"It wouldn't be right—it would be bad for Waite. I have to show him that cheating doesn't pay off."

Soren sighed, and pulled at a dry blade of buffalo grass.

"You show him from the grandstand, while he runs Big Red against Jim Carroll's Combat Third, and Auntie McCarty's Rainboy—Auntie McCarty—" Soren's voice trailed off and his sides shook with laughter. "Sounds like a school-ma'am. Bet she's a thin old maid with a skinny neck in a high shirtwaist."

Leif shut his lips tight. He thought so, too. Smiley'd shown him a letter of her's from Vermont. He took up another disc and put it in place.

"Don't jump to conclusions, Soren," he said. "Let's get this drill finished. I've got things to do, this being the last of May and the Stockman's just five weeks away."

Soren didn't say anything till they'd finished the drill and run it into the machine shed—along with all the other machinery unsold. But following Leif over to the barn to saddle the brown gelding, Smiley Brand'd had given him to ride, he burst out, "You're crazy!"

Leif went right on saddling up.

"There's three different tries been made for Big Red," Soren went on. "Waite and his gang twice. And Smiley, riding for Auntie McCarty's mares, once."

Leif pulled the cinch tight and buckled it, nodding. He hadn't known.

"That big guy's too much for you. Too fast and too smart—remember?" Soren went on.

Leif bridled the gelding and tossed the reins over his big head, then turned to Soren.

"He sure was a sight for sore eyes—standing on that knoll with the wind blowing, and the sun on his sleek red skin," Leif breathed. "I must have him, Soren. I have to beat Waite to him and win that race for Big Chris."

"And sell him, I suppose? Let some big-shot from California or Texas come up and take him right away?"

Leif hadn't thought of that before—not quite in that way. He climbed into the saddle, and then looked down at Soren. "Let's cross that bridge when we get to it," he said. "Stick around the Agency and help anyone who comes in."

Soren looked out across the town toward the foothills with their snow-filled crevices that still held the secret of McCarty's fate.

"Oh, sure," he said. "You know I'd do anything for you or your dad."

Leif grinned, then reined his horse through the gate and toward McCarty's ranch. Auntie McCarty's now, he thought with a grimace. Probably some tall thin woman, with a nose that pinched in when she got angry.

Smiley met him at the barn. Pee Wee Baker had Rainboy tied to a rope between the doors grooming him.

"Howdy, Rainboy," Leif called.

Rainboy didn't even glance at him.

"Leave him alone," Pee Wee snapped. "He's high strung." He gently smoothed Rainboy's sleek left side with a moist towel.

Smiley, who didn't like Rainboy, winked at Leif.

"Pee Wee's got him trained to a razor edge for the Stockman's," he said. "And Auntie McCarty who'll be out here for the race."

Leif couldn't get interested in Auntie's coming. All he could think of was finding Big Red before Waite could get a chance to crowd him down on that point—with capture or a fifty-foot leap into Waterton Lake and a swim across to Lost Island as the only other way out.

"She may not be so bad, Smiley," he said without conviction. "Well, I've got to roll."

"Out to Sweet Grass Run this time of night?" Smiley blurted.

"Sure," Leif nodded. "I'll be there at daylight to take him—I'll bed down tonight on the Run."

Smiley tried to stop Leif. He tried to explain that he'd go along, but the drought had tied his hands—kept him and his crew busy at the ranch.

Leif gently reined around him.

"Hey—wait a minute." Smiley went to the bunkhouse and brought out a Hudson's Bay blanket with broad red and black and white stripes. He gave Leif his own slicker and some bacon and bread.

"It gets pretty cold and makes you plenty hungry up there on Grizzly Pass," Smiley said, his eyes for once very grave.

Leif's heart began to pound. He hadn't supposed anyone but he had thought of that.

"Sure," Smiley said, matter-of-factly tying the blanket and stuff on behind Leif's saddle. "If Waite drives Big Red off the cliff and over to Lost Island the only way back is over Grizzly Pass."

Leif knew that this was so. Thirty miles over a mountain trail that led up and up and up through the mists, then along a rain-drenched one-way trail. And there was always a chance of meeting a grizzly. That's where the Pass had gotten its reputation.

"You're getting a little excited, Smiley," he said stoutly, against the feeling within him. "I'll bring Big Red in tomorrow—the easy way. Right down from Sweet Grass Run and with Waite trailing behind."

Smiley made one last effort to stop Leif.

"You haven't a prayer, Leif. Even if you take Big Red and get him to Lethbridge on time—no training, no time to teach him the ropes. And against Rainboy here who's going the mile in 1:37 flat. Forget it, kid."

Leif doggedly shook his head and moved his horse out of the gate and toward the distant rolling hills that were Sweet Grass Run.

Beyond them, the Rocky Mountains towered—Old Chief peak, and off to the left Cheney Glacier. And along its edge the tortuous trail of Grizzly Pass.

After one swift encompassing look, Leif kept his eyes on the low hills ahead. Why worry about that Pass? He was going to take Big Red this side of it.

With this in mind, and just at sundown, he rode up to the edge of Sweet Grass Run. And there on a knoll, less than a quarter of a mile away, stood Big Red.

Leif gripped his saddle horn.

"Boy," he whispered. "Boy!" His eyes went over Big Red's body, limned against the sunset. The depth of chest. The straight, short-coupled back, and the lean straight

legs of a perfect quarter-horse. "Filled out," Leif breathed.
"And built for speed." His heart leaped. If he could get
this horse, he'd have the Stockman's cinched.

With a dry feeling in his mouth, Leif softly touched his
pony's ribs and giving his low calling whistle, rode
straight for Big Red.

Big Red tossed up his head and swung to meet Leif.

A stiff evening breeze riffled his coal-black mane.
Fanned out his bushy plume tail.

Leif, riding steadily on, let his hands drop to his lariat,
uncoiling it gently.

"Hi, boy," he called. "Hi!"

Big Red pawed the ground. He raised his nose and
shrilled a snorting blast. He raced toward his mares, trotting back and forth to them, bunching them for flight.
Then stopped, stiff-legged, head in the air and brown
eyes on Leif.

Leif kept on, riding slowly. Talking, talking.

At a hundred feet, the mares started slowly drifting
toward the hills—

Leif rode steadily on, for the big horse hadn't moved.
At fifty feet, he deftly let his rope fall into a loop and
coiled the rest in his left hand.

"Easy, boy," he whispered. "We've got things to do,
boy. Big things to do for Chris. For Chris— For Chris—"
He made his voice low and coaxing.

Big Red stood as though rooted to the hills.

Leif's heart climbed into his throat. He heard his voice become a croak. It seemed that he'd hypnotized Big Red.

"Come, boy. Come, boy."

Then suddenly, his pony stumbled on a root and plunged forward. The spell between Leif and Big Red broke, and the big horse, with a shrill snort, wheeled and swept after his mares.

Leif, blinking back the tears of dismay, put his willing horse after Big Red. Through gullies, up over hills, they sped. And always Big Red and his mares stayed ahead.

This kept up till it was dark and Big Red's body was only the biggest of eleven blurred shapes fading into the murk ahead.

Leif reined in his blown horse beside a creek and dismounted.

A familiar sneering drawl almost at his elbow advised, "Better give it up, kid. Onc rider against that guy's got no chance at all."

Leif whirled to face Waite.

"Why don't you give up, too?" he demanded. "He's mine—you as good as told me so when you took Rainboy."

Waite, who had been drinking from the creek, got back on his horse.

"No horse belongs to anybody on this Run unless he's branded, Leif." Waite wiped his mouth on the back of his hand, then gathered up his reins.

Leif just stood there. It was true.

Waite rode a few feet, then turned in his saddle.

"If you want to see whose horse Big Red is, ride up to Waterton Cliff tomorrow." He laughed a short sharp laugh—like a coyote. "I've got my men staked out. We're crowdin' that big clown to the Cliff. He'll either jump or be taken."

Leif still didn't move. He was sure now that he and Big Red would ride it out together. Waite reined around to all but ride Leif down.

"And don't get any ideas about catchin' Big Red and ridin' him out from under us," Waite warned. "We're up here alone. And we'd just as soon take Big Red right out from under you as any way."

Leif looked Waite deep in the eyes.

"You wouldn't dare."

"No—who's to stop us?"

Leif shut his lips tight, and sat listening to the thud of Waite's horse fading out. When there was no sound but the splash of the creek, and the chatter of a coyote off to the right, Leif unsaddled his horse. To the sleepy twitter of birds in the willows about him, he methodically hobbled his horse. Rustling some twigs, and building a fire, he cooked four strips of bacon and ate it with some of the bread Smiley'd given him.

Then rolling up in his blanket and using his saddle for a pillow, Leif stretched out on the grass.

Had he known what lay ahead, Leif might have saddled up and ridden for Magrath. Then again he might not have. He lay staring up at the stars while a quiet strength he hadn't known he possessed flowed through him. Tomorrow, he'd take Big Red and ride him right out from under Waite. He turned on his side and slept.

CHAPTER 12

Death Dive

THE CHILL OF DAWN and a soft velvety horse nose on his cheek awakened Leif. He sat up sharply, sending two sparrows twittering madly off against the west wind.

"Big Red," he whispered, then reddened, pushing his horse's head away. "I though you were Big Red," he said ruefully.

The brown horse snorted, then dropped his head to pull at a tuft of dry grass.

Leif jumped to his feet and suddenly felt a bounding confidence.

"This is the day I'll take him," he told Brownie, while saddling and unhobbling him. "You won't mind spending a few days on the Run, will you? I'll be throwing my saddle across Big Red and streaking out of here, pronto."

Brownie tossed his head and went on grazing, while Leif quickly ate two slices of cold bacon between bread.

"There!" Leif quickly rolled his grub and blanket, tying them on behind his saddle, then led Brownie down to the creek and let the horse drink. While he, a few feet upstream, did likewise.

In five minutes he swung a leg across the cantle of his saddle and moved Brownie at a half-walk, half-trot off in the direction Waite so few hours before had taken.

Then began, as dawn changed to sunrise, to mid-morning, a duel between Leif and Waite with his riders.

Leif skirted a hill where he was sure Big Red might be. There were two Waite riders.

Big Red had been there. Now, he was a fleeing speck on the hills a mile south.

"We'll let the big guy run south," one of them jibed, twirling a handlebar moustache. "There's two riders there that'll head him."

The other rider's face broke into a swarthy grin.

Leif, without answering, swung his horse in a wide arc, and riding hard, succeeded in heading the band toward Magrath. For five miles he followed them, pressing his brown gelding to the limit.

Hope beat at him. For no Waite riders seemed in sight. Maybe he could haze the whole bunch into McCarty's corral—

Then suddenly, dipping into a swale, and coming up beyond it, he saw the band of horses stop sharply. Before Leif could more than swallow, they'd wheeled and came flying toward him. Two more of Waite's riders whooped after them.

Leif flung his rope in a wild toss

Leif braced himself. He took down his lariat and raced toward them, whirling the rope over his head and shouting.

But he was only one against two seasoned punchers.

The band swept by him in wild disorder, Big Red leading, head outstretched, pistonlike legs sending his big red body over the prairie in a smooth flowing run that was beautiful to see.

Leif flung his rope in a wild desperate toss as Big Red passed. It sang out, and out, and out. And over—

For a moment, triumph filled Leif.

"I've got him," he yelled. Swinging his pony after Big Red, he soothed, "Whoa, boy! Whoa!"

But Big Red did not slacken his pace. With five mighty bounds he stretched the rope taut against the snubbed end of Leif's saddle. Another bound and he'd snapped it like a string and sped on.

Leif pulled Brownie to a walk, ruefully coiling the frayed end of his rope.

Waite's riders swept silently past him.

That suited Leif. He was angry clear through. All right, then! He turned and rode straight as an arrow toward Waterton Cliff. No use beating around the bush, he knew as he rode along. That was where Waite would take Big Red. That was where the show-down would be.

After a mile, one of Waite's riders turned back to Leif.

"Lad," he argued, dropping alongside Leif, "what

chance have you against six hands that know their stuff?"
His deep blue eyes under a worn Stetson glowed with
concern. "Go on home and forget it."

Leif pushed on toward Waterton Cliff.

The rider pleaded, "Suppose you do snag Big Red.
Even allow you saddle him before we get there. Waite'll
just relieve you of him."

Leif did not answer. He put Brownie at a fast lope
toward Waterton Cliff. It seemed sort of crazy with Big
Red going off south again. But Leif played his hunch.

The rider made one last plea before following his partner after the fleeing horses.

"You figure to outsmart Waite," he said. "Don't try
it."

Leif rode on, his thin blond face looking straight forward, his slender body following Brownie's steady canter.

"I can see you've got an idea—maybe ride Big Red off
the Cliff," the rider persisted. "It's plumb crazy. No
horse can take that jump and make it to Lost Island."

Leif turned his head.

"I know that," he said. "But I won't have to. Big Red'll
make it up here—break through you guys circling him.
When he does, I'll be there. I'll take him and ride right
out from under your whole gang." He rode on.

The rider shaking his head and muttering, "Stubborn
kid," swerved his horse and took up the chase for Big
Red.

Leif rode on up to within a quarter of a mile of Waterton Cliff. Sitting under a big lone pine he stared out north to watch Waite's men, and Waite himself, try to corner Big Red.

Behind Leif lay Waterton Cliff. And below that the blue wind-riffled lake. Across the mile-wide lake was Lost Island. It wasn't really an island. It was a peninsula whose spruce-covered length hid the tiny thread of land connecting it with the United States land beyond.

From this United States side a trail led east along the side of Waterton Lake to the south end, then started upward, climbing toward Grizzly Pass—the only trail back to Canada and the town of Magrath.

Between watching Big Red racing his band of mares frantically from one side of the narrowing circle of Waite riders, and studying the changing cloud effects on Grizzly Pass and wondering what his chances on that Pass with Big Red might be, three hours passed by.

And then another hour, with the space left for Big Red to circulate growing less and less.

At last only the space of a quarter of a mile in diameter was left for the gallant horse.

Leif, watching from the back of Brownie, felt a sudden tightness at his midriff. In minutes now Waite would capture Big Red or else—

A fine sweat formed under Leif's hat. Scarcely knowing that he did, he wiped his forehead. And his blue eyes, deep with concern never left Big Red's flying body.

Suddenly, a half-sob escaped Leif.

Big Red and his mares had only a scant hundred feet. The seven riders made a cordon of shouting rope-swinging riders who knew just how to handle the wild horses.

"No!" Leif whispered, watching Waite take down his rope. His hands automatically clenched his own, coiled at his saddletree.

Big Red ran straight at Waite, then swerved, his forefeet flashing in the dying sun, and ran frantically for the opposite side of the ring.

Waite followed, his rope loop swinging above his head.

Leif, from his distance, drew in his breath.

The rope sang out. Missed that big red weaving head.

Leif uttered a cry, and from sheer excitement raced Brownie along the hogback.

Suddenly, he checked Brownie and stared in unbelief. But in an instant burst into a loud shout of joy.

Big Red had plunged at the riders blocking his path. His great red body toppled two of them to the ground, then swept up the slope toward Leif.

On came the horse.

Waite and his riders abandoning the mares swept in pursuit.

Leif's heart drummed against his ribs.

Hey, the big guy would be winded at the speed he'd taken. He was pulling away from his pursuers. And—

Leif's hand fell along his saddletree, the guy'd be easy to stop and saddle before Waite got there.

Leif figured out Big Red's path, then squeezed Brownie out of sight in a grove of quaking aspens, and waited.

On came Big Red.

Waite with his crew strung out behind him followed. A mile. A mile and a half.

Leif's stomach tightened under his belt, watching. It would be close, he knew. There would be a matter of seconds for him to stop Big Red and change the saddle. He reached down and loosened his cinch buckle. He loosed the throat latch on Brownie's bridle. Every move would count with Waite and his gang leaping toward them.

Now Leif could see the whites of Big Red's eyes—his distended nostrils as he ran—his coat white with lather. A moment later, he swept past Leif. And Leif, a silent prayer on his stiff lips, sent Brownie in pursuit.

Big Red turned his head questioningly, then ran on. Leif leaned forward in his saddle urging Brownie on. For a hundred yards they ran without either gaining. The Cliff loomed ahead.

Leif shoved his heels to Brownie.

"Big Red," he called. "Big Red, whoa! Whoa, boy!" The big horse sped on.

Leif gave Brownie the rope end across his rump. The

brown horse leaped forward closing the gap between
them.

He was gaining. Leif stood in his stirrups, then glanced
backward. Waite rode less than two hundred yards behind. He was mad, yelling mad, and shaking his fists in
the air as he came on.

Leif turned then, and gave Brownie the rope—

The Cliff seemed to leap at them, with Big Red leaping
straight for it.

Then, Brownie overhauled the big red horse. Leif put
out a hand for the frayed rope end he'd left on Big Red
that morning. He clutched it. Took his dallies around his
saddle horn, then set Brownie slowly to stop Big Red.

The big horse fought at first.

But Leif, running Brownie alongside, talked softly.

"Big Red—big boy. Whoa boy—"

And suddenly Big Red came to a halt.

The pound of hoofs rang from behind. Shouts filled
the air.

Leif sprang to the ground and swept the saddle from
Brownie and onto Big Red's foamy back.

Waite's voice came, "Quit it, kid. Cut it out!"

Leif swung the cinch under Big Red's heaving belly
and catching it through the cinch buckle jerked it tight.
The bridle came next with the pursuing hoofs pounding
closer.

A sob escaped Leif. Would he just get Big Red bridled

and saddled for Waite to grab? With trembling hands he slipped the bridle over Big Red's ears. Now, into the saddle. Leif grabbed the reins, his heart in his mouth.

The pounding hoofs—beating into his ears.

Leif shoved the boots to Big Red.

The big horse sprang free.

Waite surged alongside. He could just get his hands on the skirt of Leif's saddle, and clutch at the blanket.

Then the big horse's speed told. He ran straight away from Waite with Leif clinging to the saddle. But a hundred feet in the lead of Waite, Leif groaned as he swung the big horse to escape toward Magrath. For Waite's riders had fanned out and hemmed him in. Only the Cliff remained as a way of escape. The Cliff and Lost Island.

For an instant Leif hesitated. As the danger of the leap flashed through his mind, it was Waite's calling, "Run him down to the Cliff edge boys—we'll take him there!" that decided him.

Leif swung the big horse straight at the Cliff, and standing up in the stirrups watched as it seemed to come sweeping toward him.

"Chris," he breathed, against the rush of the wind, and the startled cry of Waite: "You fool. You'll kill Big Red!"

There wasn't time for more.

He caught the edge of the Cliff in his eyes, tightened his hands on the reins and gathered his body along with Big Red for the leap. And the next instant the big horse came to the brink, hesitated for an instant, then shot forward.

Leif threw his weight with him. And together, horse and rider leaped out and down.

Leif felt the swift rush of air. Heard the frantic angry shouts of Waite above. And the next instant gasped with the cold rush of water over his head.

For hours, it seemed, they struggled through the water, then suddenly broke the surface.

Leif blew out, then caught his breath.

They went down again, bobbing like a huge red apple in a giant tub.

Three times they went under, then came up. Then suddenly, the big horse righted, caught his bearing and began a lusty swim toward the green fringe of trees that was Lost Island.

Leif looked back at Waite, sitting baffled and beaten on the Cliff. Boy, that had been close. For an instant, he felt relieved. Then swinging back to face the Island forgot his relief in what lay ahead. Cautiously then, he slid from Big Red's back off over his rump and catching hold of his tail, let the horse tow him toward Lost Island.

Climbing to the sandy shore and shaking the water from his clothes, Leif looked south and up at mist-drenched Grizzly Pass. A new sure light filled his eyes as he unsaddled Big Red and spread his blanket out to dry.

"Tomorrow, Big Red," he said to the horse, standing

Together horse and rider leaped out and down

dripping and blown by the lake edge, "we'll go over that Pass. Then on to Lethbridge to win the Stockman's—"

Big Red shook his head to clear the mane of water, then raising it snorted, reared and plunged off up the Island.

Leif, turning to see what had stampeded Big Red, came face to face with a Grizzly she-bear and two trailing cubs. The three came right at him, and they meant business—

CHAPTER 13

Grizzly Pass

LEIF WAITED, intently eying the bears coming toward him. He was surprisingly calm. He'd been through too much to stop now—to let these bears stop him from getting Big Red to that race. He stooped to grasp a stark-white driftwood club and came up full of fight.

But a firm voice off to the right commanded, "Give ground—she only wants your provisions."

Leif reluctantly backed toward the lake.

It seemed the man was right. For the old bear, paying no attention to Leif, stalked to the saddle and with one swipe of her paw laid the contents of Leif's roll wide open for the cubs.

"You!" Leif burst out. He had to have that grub to get over Grizzly Pass. And now the cubs were licking it up.

"No," the voice warned. "Back off—and don't get between the mother bear and her cubs."

Leif backed still farther, while the smaller of the two cubs thrust his head through a hole in Leif's blanket. "My blanket!" he wailed, then burst out laughing. The cub surely did look funny streaking for the woods with the blanket sailing out behind.

"Quite humorous," the voice said, as the mother bear and the other cub raced after the distressed one in the lead.

Leif turned toward a dark lean man in a United States Forest Ranger uniform.

"I'm Joe Causley," he said, riding a slim bay mare out from the sheltering spruce.

Leif had heard about Joe—about his perfect English and how he lived here in the mountains with his mare, Bess.

"I know," Leif nodded. "I heard about you saving that tenderfoot's life on Grizzly Pass last year."

"I was most happy to come to his assistance at an embarrassing moment," Joe said, with a slow smile.

Leif smiled with him, then suddenly remembered.

"My horse," he burst out. "I've got to catch him—got to."

"Assuredly." Causley took his left foot from his stirrup and motioned Leif to get up behind. "We'll head for the neck of land."

Leif sprang up behind Causley's lean body, and they

sped through the trees and out to the little neck of bare
ground that connected Lost Island with the mainland of
Glacier Park.

There, head erect and poised for flight, stood Big Red.

Leif slipped from Causley's mare and started walking
slowly toward Red. All the months of struggle to get the
horse for the race seemed centered right here. Just let Big
Red streak into the woods and it might take months to
get him back—

Leif opened his lips stiff with panic and whistled,
softly—a low coaxing whistle.

Something of that memory of the blizzard must have
flowed into Big Red's mind. He turned his sleek head
toward Leif and stood silent and rooted on his huge
black hoofs while Leif walked up and took hold of his
bridle reins.

"Whew!" Leif leaned against that satin coat and
stared off at Grizzly Pass. "Don't ever do that again, Big
Red."

The horse nuzzled his jumper collar.

Suddenly, a flash of lightning off beyond Grizzly Pass
searched out the snowy crannies of Ahern Glacier.

"Some precipitation of water is imminent," Causley
said, pushing Bess close to Leif. "Traverse of Grizzly
Pass will be impossible because of snow for a week—but
you will be my guest. Accompany me, please."

Going back to put his scarred saddle on Big Red, then

mounting to follow Causley, Leif didn't want to be stubborn. But—"I'm going over Grizzly Pass tomorrow," he said as they left the Island behind.

Causley, on his mare, led the way along the side of Waterton to his cabin under the shadow of Grizzly Pass. Even then, he did not reply to Leif, but waited till they'd put their horses in the log barn and unsaddled before he spoke.

At length he said gravely, "No. It would be too hazardous. The trail is precipitous and narrow. One misstep and your horse will tumble a thousand feet into the lake. Then there is always the chance of encountering an Ursus Horribilus."

"And a worse chance of Big Chris meeting Culp Horribilus," Leif blurted. "Or Bankruptancy Terribilus."

To Joe Causley's stare, Leif replied by leaning up against Big Red's stall and telling him about the jam Chris was in. And how Big Red was going to win the Stockman's and pull him out. When he'd finished, Joe looked at him solemnly and said, "Assuredly—you must go over Grizzly Pass tomorrow. To tell your father you are without harm. And to prepare Big Red for the Stockman's Racing."

As his words died away, Big Red coughed—a deep hollow cough, and nuzzled his left forefoot just above the hoof.

Leif's eyes met Causley's in panicky question. Would

Big Red make it over the Pass tomorrow—or even later in time for the Stockman's?

They led the big horse out into the runway of the barn, where they could examine him.

"Some lake water on the lungs—acquired when he dived," Causley said. "And the foot—a sprain that won't heal too soon." His eyes, slow and thoughtful, met Leif's. "You will be my guest till the healing is complete."

"But Father!" Leif whispered. "He'll worry. And I've got to train Big Red."

Causley looked out through the barn door to the trees that seemed each to be his special friend.

"In the morning, or the next, or the one following, we shall see," he said.

And the third morning they did see. For through the giant spruce came Soren, out into the clearing. He was on foot. Grinning and tickled to find Leif okay.

"Left my horse and mooched around the end of the lake," he explained. "Had to come searching—you ready to go home, Leif?"

Leif led the way to the barn, and pointed to Big Red's foot.

"Not till just time for the Stockman's, if then?" he said. "But, brother, am I glad to see you. You can go back and tell Big Chris, I'm okay—" His breath caught. Then came again. "And, tell him," he said, softly, "that I'll be in time for the Stockman's."

"Assuredly." Causley nodded. "But now, I invite you to breakfast."

They moved toward the cabin from which blue smoke curled into the crisp morning air. And inside to bacon and round browned hot cakes with wild honey.

By ten o'clock Soren, still smiling, still with that light of devotion in his eyes for Leif, waddled toward the line of trees at the edge of the clearing. Then with a last wave of his hand, and a shout, "I'll tell Chris that you're okay," he moved out of sight.

"And that I'll be there for the race," Leif called after him, with more assurance than he felt.

For it didn't look too good—with Big Red favoring his forefoot. And still coughing—

Leif doggedly settled down to nurse his horse. A week passed—two—then more weeks. Till finally there was no more time—it was the day before the Stockman's.

Leif saddled his red horse in silence. Then led him over the barn-door sill to the cold morning air.

Causley led his bay mare out and climbed on.

Leif settled into the saddle, his eyes lifted to Grizzly Pass, half-hidden by racing clouds. A sharp wind blew from the west.

"Well, let us proceed," Causley said, gathering up his reins. "I will take you over Grizzly Pass.

But suddenly, off along the road they'd come a few short weeks before, rose a slow spiral of smoke.

"Ah—" Causley swung in his saddle. "A conflagration among the spruce," he said sharply. Suddenly words flung from his wide brown lips. "Ride straight to the summit, Leif," he ordered. "Don't delay. It is raining up there now. By afternoon it may turn to snow."

The smoke seemed to swell, and Causley started Bess sharply up the trail. "If you meet an Ursus or, I mean a bear," he threw back to Leif, "slide off your horse and climb up the cliffs—if you can."

"And leave Big Red to be killed?" Leif called.

Causley's voice came faintly now. He'd started to trot Bess. "Better that than both," he called. "Farewell Leif." And he was gone.

Leif couldn't see himself climbing up a cliff and leaving Big Red to face a bear. "The thing to do was to go right on through," he told himself with a wry grin. "Give old Ursus Horribilus the eye and take the trail for Lethbridge."

With his back very straight, but a funny feeling up it just the same, Leif gently touched Big Red with his boot heels and rode east a mile, then, at a fork in the trail turned left and began to climb. He was on Grizzly Pass trail at last.

"Okay, boy, this is it," he said, resisting a desire to turn back. Maybe Causley needed help with that blaze anyway? But there was Big Chris' anxious face before him. Leif kept Big Red at a steady climb.

For an hour they rose, the air getting thin around him, and cold. Leif let Big Red wind a moment.

Off to the left and down lay the blue ribbon that was Waterton Lake. And beyond, the Cliff, and beyond that the sloping foothills leading to the prairie and Magrath.

Leif pressed Big Red on.

But contrarily, the big horse took a notion to go back. He fretted as they climbed. And his coat in spite of the chill wind, lathered.

Leif held him to a steady climb.

"Come on," he whispered. In the lonesomeness his voice struck the icy ledge beside him and came sharply back.

Big Red moved on, and up till the mist surrounded them. Till the trail, a narrow, tortuous mist-drenched thing wound around still sharper rocky ledges. Till Leif thought the next ledge would be the last and the trail would have reached the summit, and start dropping to safety.

"It's got to be sometime," he said to Red, who tossed his head and again tried to swerve.

Leif forced him on.

That next ledge two hundred feet up would surely be the summit. "A rock shaped like an Ursus Horribilus— from which the Pass acquires its cognomen," Causley had said.

But it wasn't a rock shaped like a bear. It was just an-

other ledge that squeezed Big Red as he passed, and led
to a part of the trail that narrowed to almost nothing.

Leif squeezed to the saddle listening to the steady beat
of Big Red's hoofs on the rocks.

Suddenly, as if the narrowed trail weren't enough, the
mist around him turned to rain. And another five hundred feet up, to snow. Tiny icy flakes bit into Leif's numb
white face. And down along his right, way down, came
the shrill sigh of a chasm breeze.

Leif felt the up-rush of the wind, tasting the cold icy
snow that came with it. And suddenly through the sleet
ahead, his eyes made out a rock—Grizzly Rock for sure.

"The summit! Big Red, the summit!"

Big Red stopped stock-still on the trail and tossed his
nose in the air with a snort.

"It's just a rock—" Leif started to say, then felt the
words die in his throat. For the rock was moving—and
down to meet him.

Big Red started backing up.

The bear moved on all fours toward them, growling.

Big Red tried to turn on the trail.

The rocky wall bumped his rear, and his forefeet hung
on the edge of the precipice. He straightened, and tried
to climb the ledge beside him. His foot bit the rocks and
could find no footing. Once more, Big Red faced the on-
coming bear.

Leif glanced frantically up the ledge Big Red had tried

to climb. By standing in the saddle, he could leap to safety—and let Big Red take it alone.

Grimly, Leif deepened in his saddle and warily watched the bear close the gap between them.

Now the bear reared on his haunches. A grizzly all right. Leif could see the silver-tipped hair along his neck.

Big Red screamed.

Leif yelled, "Beat it! Beat it!"

From across the chasm from another rocky point his words echoed back, "Beat—it! Beat—it!"

The bear moved slowly forward.

Leif could see his little black eyes shining from the short fur around them, and he sensed that it was all over with him and Big Red.

"Big Chris," he whispered. "So long, Dad."

He sat in the saddle, bracing himself for the impact of a mighty swipe from that upraised paw. No, that wasn't the way. If he had to die, he'd die fighting. With a shout, he jerked Big Red's reins taut and put the big red horse right at the bear.

Ten feet, five—the distance closed between them.

The bear seemed to straighten. A low deep growl surged from his half-opened mouth. He lunged forward with upraised paws.

Big Red reared to meet him. A shrill scream came from him. His big hoofs beat the air. Like mighty pile drivers they moved rhythmically forward.

The bear swiped with his left paw.

Leif felt the reins jerked from his hands. Saw the bridle leap from Big Red's head.

Again the big horse screamed. His feet came down. And with a mighty rush struck the bear flat on his head, hauling him to the trail, then over the ledge.

He disappeared from sight, a mighty ball of squirming rumbling fur. Down, down, down, till there was no sound but the uprush of snow-laden air and the labored breathing of the big red horse.

Leif shaking, hardly knowing what he did, slipped from Big Red to gather up the bridle. He patched it as well as he could, put it on Big Red's head again and climbed back into the saddle.

The big horse moved forward—over the summit and on down to the prairie and the trail leading toward Lethbridge. It was late evening, and the big horse moved with a limp. It would mean most of the night riding. Entering the race with a deep flesh wound along his shoulder. Big Red did not falter.

Leif, on his back, straightened and rode with him. To win the race was the thing. To win the race for Big Chris. Horse and rider moved on till it was dark, and then on, and on, toward the distant lights that gleamed so far away, and seemed to grow larger so slowly.

The bear swiped with his left paw

CHAPTER 14

Losing Race

LEIF RODE BIG RED down a back street of Leth-bridge the next afternoon. Boys followed him, yelling. "Hey, look at the tramp."

Others on the opposite sidewalk on their way to the Fair took it up. "Tramp! Tramp! Kid tramp on a big red horse—hey guy, when'd you have a bath?"

Leif rode on, pushing straight toward the big white grandstand that loomed over the housetops. He guessed he did look like a tramp all right. But what really worried him was Big Red's cough that hadn't left him. What about that bear-claw wound on his shoulder? Would it affect his speed?

He moved down the back street, circled the town and out across the strip of prairie to go through the gate and up to the contestant barns.

From there, he could look across the way and see his father's exhibit of farm machinery. Good old Chris. He hadn't missed an exhibit in fifteen years of running the I.H.C. agency.

But suddenly, Lief reached a trembling hand down to steady himself by Big Red's mane. His lips formed the words, but his head couldn't take it in.

"No exhibit," he mouthed, staring at the empty space.

"That's right, Leif!" Soren came up. "We had a fire at Magrath. The warehouse went up in smoke. Jensen the blockman was there, and Mr. Culp. I guess Culp's got the Agency from Big Chris at last."

Leif steadied himself. A fire. The one thing needed to put Chris out of business. Well, it really was up to him now. Chris had come through for him so often. Two thousand dollars would save the Agency. Get things going again. Leaping to the ground, he led Big Red down the alley of box stalls.

Big Jim Carroll came out of one, and after a quick stare at Leif, moved anxiously toward him.

"Lad," he said, gently. "You better lie down. You're out on your feet."

Leif shook Carroll's hand from his shoulder.

"Got to get Big Red in shape for the race," he said, leading Big Red into an empty stall and starting to unsaddle him. He was glad Jim Carroll didn't laugh.

But Pee Wee Parker, coming through the box-stall door, did.

"That's a hot one," he said, eying Big Red. "So this is the clown colt? The horse that's going to run Rainboy right off the track? Boy, will Auntie McCarty get a kick out of that."

Leif grinned. His head felt light. But there was no time to eat till after the race.

"All right for Auntie McCarty then," he said, but the words didn't mean anything.

Pee Wee was saying. "Sure, they found McCarty dead, up in Earthquake Fault. He had a will on him and it's to be read today after the race. But Auntie's here running the shebang already. She's going to see me take the Stockman's in a breeze."

Jim Carroll stopped Pee Wee by shoving him out of the stall.

"It's a fact, Leif. Pee Wee's right—you haven't got a chance. You've ridden all night, haven't you?"

Leif shook his head, while that urge filled him. He couldn't breathe. It was like something of weight that had to be lifted. And the only way it could be lifted was to get on the track astride Big Red, and win—

"No." He shook his head. "I slept in a hay stack two hours. Big Red ate plenty of hay. A lady found me and gave me a glass of milk and a sandwich. What time is it?"

"Two o'clock," Carroll said.

"Two o'clock—" Leif caught at the manger of the stall and hung on till his head cleared. "In half an hour—"

He grasped Carroll's hand and led him over to Big
Red. "Listen?" he said, leaning down to put an ear to
the big horse's lungs. "Got lake water in 'em when he
jumped off Waterton Cliff."

Carroll's eyes bulged. But at Leif's motioning hands,
he stooped down and listened.

"Not good," he said, straightening to meet Leif's
anxious eyes. "Not good, but he can run—"

Leif thought Carroll would never finish.

"Yes, he can run—it won't injure him. But it'll cut
his staying qualities. Give it up, Leif. You haven't a
chance."

"Sure, give it up." Soren came in with a hamburger for
Leif. "Here, eat this. We'll go sit in the stands along with
Auntie McCarty and Anna. Chris'll be with us, too, in
about an hour. He had to be with Turner out at the
Agency to go over the burned stuff. Them and Culp."

Leif could see Big Chris patiently going over the
ruined equipment with Turner and big, bluff Culp waiting to grab the Agency.

Leif grasped the sandwich and took spare bites.
Enough to keep his head clear and not make any extra
weight for Big Red in the coming race. That done, he got
a currycomb and brush and began grooming Big Red's
sweat-caked body.

"You've no racing saddle, Leif," Soren pointed out.

Leif's hands stopped running the brush along Big Red's back. It was a fact.

A grim look came on Carroll's face, standing there in the stall.

From the grandstand came the fading shouts of people watching the wind-up of the calf-roping—the last event before the Stockman's Race.

Carroll turned to Leif. "Who runs this race?" He demanded. "Who started it in the first place?"

Leif, puzzled, blurted, "Why, why, I guess you and McCarty did."

Carroll's big sunburned face set with decision.

"Then McCarty's heir and I can add a new rule—we'll ride stock-saddles today."

Pee Wee came running down the alley.

"Nix," he shrilled, looking like a little white bantam rooster. "It's an outrage—Rainboy's never had a stock-saddle on. I'll go an' see Auntie." He stalked out the door and headed for the grandstand.

"I'll go see her, myself," Carroll said, moving after Pee Wee.

Leif walked out of Big Red's stall and down to where Rainboy, blanketed in a red and white checked blanket to his erect gentlemanly ears, stood staring haughtily into space.

"Hello, guy," Leif whispered through the door.

Rainboy didn't move his head—didn't bat an eye.

Leif with a rueful smile walked back to Big Red's stall and went on with his grooming. He fetched a bucket with some warm water and washed out the bear wound, already starting to heal.

"Red," he said, gently. "I guess anything Carroll and Auntie decide won't be unfair to Rainboy—the slick geezer."

Big Red nosed Leif's thin shoulder, then turned his head to watch Carroll come in.

"Couldn't find Auntie," Carroll admitted, as Pee Wee, grinning to show tiny sharp teeth, passed the stall. "And—" his voice trailed lamely off as the loudspeaker blared, "Next event, ladies and gentlemen—the Stockman's Race for local horses. No prize. Contestants, Combat Third, Jim Carroll's entry; Rainboy, Auntie McCarty's entry; and a surprise entry, Big Red—owned by Leif Olson."

A shout greeted this announcement, followed by an excited buzz of curiosity from the stands.

The announcer went on, "As is customary, the winner will be sold to the highest bidder immediately after the race."

A small burst of handclapping followed this last announcement, then expectant silence.

Leif, his heart hammering, walked up to untie Big Red.

Whitey Baker, Carroll's rider for Combat Third, rode the big brown horse out of the alley and across the runway leading to the track.

A small group of men with intent faces parted to let him pass.

"Buyers," Soren came in beside Leif, to whisper. "From Californy and Texas. They're loaded with dough."

Leif put the patched, bear-clawed bridle on Big Red, then pulled his foretop down to wipe his tired eyes. Boy, he had to win this race.

Rainboy, with Pee Wee up, minced daintily out past Big Red's stall, turning to give the big horse a sharp mocking nicker as he passed.

It was that nicker that burned Leif up. He stood silent a moment, then suddenly with trembling hands led Big Red out of the stall to the alley.

"Boost, Soren," he said, lifting his foot.

"But, you got no saddle."

"Boost," Leif repeated. "I'm a lot heavier than Pee Wee or Whitey. It'll be only fair that I ride bareback."

Soren shaking his head, put a fat hand on Leif's ankle and boosted him to Big Red's back.

Leif picked up the reins and with a gentle nudge moved Big Red out the alley and after the big brown Combat Third and the little prancing show-off, Rainboy.

"Whew! What is this?" He heard as he passed the knot of buyers.

"A horse," one man said.

A low whistle came from another—a small man in a gray suit, with sunburned face and shrewd gray eyes.

"Murphy, from Santa Barbara," Soren whispered, trotting along beside Leif. "Win this—if they'll let you, and he'll pay plenty for Big Red."

Soren's voice was cut short by the clipped voice of Murphy.

"Just a moment, boy."

He came up to Leif who stopped impatiently, and ran a deft hand down Big Red's front legs. "Oh-oh, what's this?" His eyes fell on the bear wound on Big Red's shoulder.

"Bear claws," Leif said. "I've got to go, sir."

"Bear claws, indeed?" Murphy's sparse eyebrows raised.

In the general amusement of the other buyers, he backed away and let Leif ride on.

But looking back, Leif saw the group come together and look after Big Red. A bit of conversation floated to him over the distant buzzing of the packed stands: "If that horse is as fast as he looks, he's for me."

"Winter, from Texas," Soren whispered, walking along. "He's worth ten millions—and breeds quarter horses."

Leif nodded and moved out on to the track. He looked up at the stands. Felt their hush, then heard the buzzing of excitement as they glimpsed Big Red.

Leif thought everything would be all right.

But suddenly, the announcer said, "Just a moment—a slight delay." And the three judges in their little white tower put their heads together, with an occasional glance at Big Red.

Carroll came walking across the track and up to Leif.

"It's dangerous," he said. "And you won't make a race of it—no purchase. You'll jerk Big Red's mouth at the getaway—"

A voice from the stands said softly, with a broad Norwegian accent, "He bane good boy, on good horse. Let him run—" Her voice trailed off in sheer terror that she'd dared to speak.

"Anna!" Leif's face reddened clean down inside his stained leather jumper.

But Anna's words were the one thing needed by the crowd.

A cheer went up for Leif and Big Red.

"Let him run!" swelled the cry. "Let the big red run!"

"Big Red!" Anna called.

"Big Red!" the crowd roared.

Carroll turned to the judges. To the stands, then with a shrug opened his palms and motioned for the race to proceed.

Leif moved after the other two horses to the starting line.

Passing the stands, he looked up into them. Big Chris must be there some place? And Auntie McCarty—probably a funny-looking old thing. He wondered if she looked like McCarty.

Then, he reached the starting line.

Rainboy had the pole position—leave it to him. Then, Combat Third, and on the outside, Big Red.

Combat fought his bit, reared and turned his brown rump square away from the tape.

Rainboy, the perfect gentleman, stood looking down the track.

Big Red tossed his head, stretched his neck, and suddenly cocked his ears toward a fleecy cloud.

Combat straightened half-around. A little more and they'd be away—

A hush settled over the stands.

Leif pulled Big Red's head down, then leaned forward along his black mane.

"Watch, Red," he whispered.

"Sure, watch," Pee Wee sneered. "Watch our smoke at the finish."

Suddenly, Combat faced the track.

Rainboy grew deadly quiet, and in the silence, the tape shot up—they were off!

Rainboy shot forward.

Combat watched him racing for the turn.

Big Red's lunge all but unseated Leif. He caught at Big Red's mane, but his left bridle-hand jerked Big Red's mouth. By the time he'd gotten his balance, Big Red trailed Combat and Rainboy by five lengths.

As they passed the grandstand, Rainboy, always the show-off, jumped into the lead. Combat fought every foot of the way, but the little bay colt pulled away.

Big Red, with Leif sitting low along his mane, pounded along, still five lengths behind.

On the back stretch Leif shook Big Red's reins.

"Come on, boy," he breathed.

The big horse leaped forward. But suddenly dropped back. His eyes took on a glazed look, and his breathing sounded harsh. He lost another length.

Taking the turn into the stretch, Leif saw Rainboy streaking for the finish. Little Rainboy that Waite had taken from him. The horse that by rights was his. A sense of the unfairness of it all came over Leif. Big Chris' taut face there among the embers of his ruined business swam before his eyes.

Suddenly, Leif leaned forward and did a thing that would bring Red out—bring him to the fore or send him bucking crazy-mad off across the rail fence and into the mid-field. He ran his thumbs along under Big Red's mane and dug in hard.

Leif felt the big horse tremble. Felt the outrage course through that big frame.

Then suddenly Big Red leaped forward. His long head shot out. In half a hundred strides, he pulled even with Combat.

The stands shouted, "Big Red! Big Red!"

But there was Rainboy, a small bay streak, in the lead and speeding for the finish. Not a wasted move deflected him. The machine-runner, the little sleek bay ran like he'd been shot from a catapult.

Leif leaned low over Big Red's mane. He waited, feeling the big red horse running his heart out.

Now Big Red pulled even with Rainboy—Combat had been left behind.

Leif's eyes dimmed. The course ahead wobbled. He sensed a hush from the stands. That meant Big Red was losing. Leif felt the bitter taste of defeat in his throat. Knew with searing surety that he'd failed Big Chris. Then suddenly, reaching back to that day in the stands, when that crazy idea'd first popped into his head, Leif leaned forward and with those big ears bobbing before him, whispered in words that were almost a prayer, "Run, Big Red— Red horse, run!"

The effect was magical. With a bound the big horse shot forward, and with an agonising burst of sheer power, shot over the line—a winner.

Riding back to the finish line, Leif leaned down and

Leif felt the big horse tremble

brushed wet eyes along Big Red's stiff mane. "Red—" His lips trembled. "Red horse, you really ran—"

He rode into the circle of men gathered before the judges stand and jumped lightly down. Happily he turned around, then anguish hit him like the blow of a mallet. For there, facing him and impatiently waiting for Big Red's sale, stood Winters and Murphy.

"Yes, you really ran," Leif whispered dully to Big Red. "Ran yourself right out of my life—"

Suddenly, standing there, with Big Red nosing his chest with that big soft nose of his, Leif knew that he could never give up Big Red. That someway, somehow, he'd have to find a way to get Big Chris out and keep Big Red as well—

CHAPTER 15

Big Red's Sale

HALF AN HOUR LATER they were back in the barn. Leif, munching on a hot dog, sat on an overturned feed bucket watching Big Red drink cool water from a bucket Smiley patiently held for him.

Boy, did he feel low! Big Red to be sold in a few minutes. Sure, he'd bring at least two thousand—maybe more. It would be enough to take him and Big Chris away and set them up some place else.

Big Jim Carroll came in, and with him, a girl—a slim dark girl in riding clothes with a scarlet shirt and freckles on her nose.

"Well, Leif," Jim said, moving in beside Big Red. "Some horse—he'll bring plenty."

Leif nodded. And that pain hit him again. He had to keep Big Red and get money for Big Chris, too.

"Yes," he said softly, eying the girl—probably a pupil of Auntie McCarty's. He wished she'd stayed outside.

Suddenly he got up and walked in beside Big Red, and before he knew it the stall was full of boys. Walter Culp,

Jimmy Larsen, Ronald Swanson, the Boy Rangers. Anna, outside the door, stood pink cheeked and wide-eyed.

"Ol' guy, ol' pal," the boys exclaimed, swarming over Big Red. Suddenly, they began to bawl.

Leif's throat felt dry.

The girl was looking, not saying anything.

Murphy came in, all business, and with a strange man with cold blue eyes and a little black bag.

Leif instantly disliked him.

"Mind if I have my veterinarian look him over before the sale?" Murphy snapped. "Seemed to me his wind sounded funny. And that bear claw?"

It gave Leif the creeps. The guy acted as though he already owned Big Red. Leif got a picture of darkness coming on, and the stall empty. Of Big Red hustled into a stock car and going clean to California. Never to be seen again.

Leif said, dully, "Okay, Mr. Murphy." Then told the boys to go. "Used to swim with them," he explained, then reddened at Murphy's thin smile, and the girl's stare.

"All that nonsense is past for Big Red, now," Murphy snapped.

The veterinarian went over Big Red, shaking his head, running his hand down Big Red's legs, and cocking his head to one side.

Big Chris drove up and came into the barn. And Turner—trailed by Culp.

It was all over. Culp as good as had the Agency, Leif could tell. Turner, hating to do it, would have no other alternative than to turn it over unless Big Red was sold and the money plunked down to the I.H.C. But Leif felt that same stubbornness. He didn't want to sell Big Red—

"Leif," Big Chris said softly. "Sorry not to have seen the race."

Leif's heart swelled. Not a word about himself. About the fire and the way he'd been stripped of fifteen years' effort. His only thought was of Leif.

Leif felt anger at himself. If he were any good he'd figure a way out of this thing.

"Yeah, it was a good race, Dad," he said. "Big Red was wonderful."

"Wonderful!" the girl said, moving toward Leif.

Smiley shook his head and held her back.

The veterinarian finished examining Big Red, nodding to Murphy and smiling.

"He's sound—sound as a dollar," he said.

"Anybody could tell that without a ten-dollar vet, Murphy," Winter boomed, coming through the door.

"Precisely," Murphy said, then turned to Leif. "Let's get this thing over. I want to ship my horse out on to-night's freight."

Leif saw the girl glance at Smiley. And Smiley shake

his head. He wondered what was going on? But whatever it was, things were closing in on him. And again, he knew that someway, somehow, he had to keep Big Red. That little icebox Murphy couldn't have him. Nor windbag Winter either.

Soren came edging into the stall, to pick at Leif's elbow.

"You'd better start the sale," he warned, looking deep into Leif's smouldering eyes.

Leif didn't more than half-listen. If only Carroll could buy Big Red. But Carroll had been hit by the drought, too.

"Yeah, Soren," he said, at last. "I guess so."

"Well, let's get going then," Murphy snapped, pulling out a thin black pen to finger in his dry hands.

Winter nodded.

Jim Carroll moved over to Leif.

"I'm not bidding," he said, gently. "Want me to act for you, Leif?"

Leif swallowed and stared around.

Big Chris had moved over to stand with Turner. They talked in low tones, Turner's thin face a study in perplexity.

Suddenly, Leif had an idea. He'd go out and find Auntie McCarty. McCarty's will must have been read by now. He'd explain to her what a swell horse Big Red was. And how much money she had, and how they could go into partnership—cross Big Red with some of McCarty's mares. It would be a working agreement with the only string attached that she buy all her equipment from I.H.C.—from Big Chris. That would force Turner to let him keep the Agency.

He said, "Just a moment. Just wait one minute," then slipped through the stall door and over to the Fun Zone. And there, he saw a woman that must be Auntie McCarty. Wearing a white starched shirtwaist she was just raising a glass of pink lemonade to her thin lips.

Leif walked up to her and, taking off his hat, blurted, "I'm Leif Olson, Auntie McCarty. And you've got to buy Big Red. He'll raise a lot of swell colts—"

The lady choked and put her glass down.

"I, I mean, he's a stallion, and you've got a lot of mares—" Leif plunged on.

Suddenly, the lady's long arms flung into the air.

"Indeed—" she shrilled. Her voice raised. "Help! Police!"

Leif moved sadly away. He guessed she wasn't Auntie after all.

He tried two others after that. Both ladies in shirt-waists.

One just turned her back, after a quick stare, and the other slapped his face. Then, at the dazed expression on it, burst into tears.

"Oh, you dear boy," she exclaimed and kissed him.

Leif went back to the barn. He was licked.

"About time," snapped Murphy, looking sharply at a chromium watch on his thin hairy wrist. "If this sale doesn't click in ten seconds, I'm not bidding—"

"Hurray!" applauded Winter, then turned to Leif. "Take your time, young man."

Leif nodded. And suddenly he saw the girl and Smiley. They'd moved out of the stall and stood down in front of Rainboy's box. Leif moved down to them, a foolish feeling running through him. Why hadn't he thought of them before?

"I've got to find Auntie McCarty," he said earnestly.

Smiley snickered.

"Why?" the girl asked, frowning at Smiley, then raising her eyes to Leif's.

"Because—" Leif said, and then told her about Big Chris and Red. And what a horse like Big Red could do for McCarty's racing stock.

"Sort of a memorial to Mr. McCarty?" the girl suggested, her eyes shining.

Leif nodded. "Sure, that's it. But first we've got to find Auntie and get her to bid Big Red in."

"There was another member to this will," the girl said. Her eyes fixed meaningly on Leif's. "Somebody who did McCarty a wonderful service just before he died—taught him a new meaning of life. A kindly meaning— Do you think he'd want Big Red, too?"

Leif paused, "Maybe, but this Auntie— Let's get her first."

"I mean," the girl persisted. "Put yourself in this boy's, I mean man's, place as a partner to Auntie. What would you do?"

Leif's blue eyes shone.

"Boy, there's no argument there," he said. "I'd buy him."

"Then we'll go find Auntie and talk it over," the girl said. "Come on, Smiley."

They moved out of the barn as Leif made no move to start the sale. Murphy put his pen back in the pocket of his light-tan gabardine suit.

"Very well." He nodded to his vet. "For me, the sale is off." He started to leave the barn.

Leif, his heart in his mouth, watched him go.

"Start her up," Soren pleaded, picking at Leif's sleeve.

Jim Carroll looked at Leif, then at Winter, then back to Leif.

"If Murphy leaves," his manner said. "Then Winter'll have the bidding all his own way—he'll buy Big Red at his own price."

Leif calculated the chances of Smiley and the girl finding Auntie. He looked across at Big Chris, and got no help there. Big Chris as usual was letting Leif make his own decision.

At length, Leif took a deep breath and stopped the retreating Murphy cold.

"Start the sale, Mr. Carroll," he said.

"That's better," Murphy snapped, coming back. "And I'll bid two thousand dollars to start"—and to finish this Texas Windbag, Winter, his manner indicated.

Winter took out a big gold watch and began to spin it in front of his pearl gray vest.

"Twenty-five hundred for the big red boy," he said easily.

Leif gulped, and stared at Murphy. Wasn't the little guy going to keep on bidding? He had to, to give the girl and Smiley time to find Auntie. They'd gone on with a hurried, "We'll be back in time, Leif."

Murphy said, "Humpf!" He took out his pen, twiddling it in his thin dry fingers.

"Do I hear a further bid, gentlemen?" Carroll asked. "If not—"

Leif's heart almost stopped. His eyes flew to the barn door through which the girl and Smiley had gone looking for Auntie.

"Hurry up, Auntie," he breathed. "Hurry up—"

"Going— Going at twenty-five hundred, to Mr. Winter," Carroll sang out.

Leif felt his spine tingle. Something clutched his midriff. Big Red sold to Texas—to a big guy who didn't care too much about horses. Just a big guy throwing his money around. Leif moved over to Murphy.

"He's worth more than that," he said. "He's a swell horse."

Murphy snapped, "Mind your own business." Then bending over to talk to his vet, he added, "Twenty-seven fifty."

Leif breathed again, his eyes moving again to the barn door.

"Three thousand," Winter exploded. "I'll make a Texan out of that big red boy. Maybe a rodeo outlaw."

"Thirty-three fifty," snapped Murphy.

"Thirty-five," said Winter.

"Thirty-seven fifty," Murphy nodded.

"Four thousand." A line of red ran up Winter's bull neck.

"Forty-five hundred." Murphy's face went dead white.

Leif caught hold of the side of the box stall. Forty-five hundred dollars. It was a lot of money.

Carroll's eyes sought Leif's. They said, "I've got to stop this some place."

Leif couldn't breathe. His eyes felt as though they'd popped out and lay on his stiff cheeks. He started to nod assent to Carroll, when across the sill stepped Smiley and the girl. And no one was with them. No stiff tall woman in a white shirtwaist who might be Auntie McCarty and save Big Red from going out of his life.

Leif knew then that he was licked. Sure, he and Big Chris would have money. But he'd had a hunch he could have money for Big Chris and Big Red to keep, as well.

Leif swung toward Carroll to give him the sign to sell Big Red to either Winter or Murphy. And sell quick.

But the girl held up her hand. "Just a minute," she said.

Leif turned to her. "You didn't find her?" he asked. "This Auntie?"

She shook her head. "No old Auntie," she said.

Leif groaned. "And the other party to McCarty's will? I suppose he was missing too?"

Smiley snickered, but the girl's eyes on him, silenced the rider.

"He—he knows you—this other party to the will," she said, turning to Leif. "He'll do whatever you say." She swallowed, then went on. "You're to bid as high as you have to go to get Big Red."

Leif felt the barn start to whirl. Something took hold of him and seemed to shake him. It was crazy, plum crazy. And she'd talked to Auntie.

"Does Auntie agree to this?"

The girl nodded, then held a handkerchief to her mouth and seemed to go into a fit of coughing.

Leif turned to Carroll and snapped, "For the McCarty heirs, I am empowered to bid five thousand dollars for Big Red."

Murphy, without a single backward glance, stepped like a little gray dandy from the barn.

Winter, plopping his watch into its nest, followed Murphy.

In the silence that followed, Carroll's voice briskly asked, "Any other bids?" Then, after a moment, he added, "Sold—to the heirs of the McCarty estate."

"To Leif and me—" the girl said.

And that seemed to let pandemonium loose in the barn.

Smiley thumped Leif on the back.

The stall filled with boys swarming over Big Red.

And there, too, stood Big Chris.

Leif drew a hand across his eyes and faced the laughing girl.

The girl laughed again. A laugh that told Leif what he should have guessed long since.

He gulped, then said, "You're Auntie!"

She nodded, her brown eyes brimming.

"Spelled A-n-t-i-e—it's a nickname for Antoinette."

Leif reddened and could think of but one thing to say.

"You've bought a swell horse," he finally managed.

Antoinette laughed again. It was like cold clear water running over stones.

"Yes, we have—" she said gently.

"We?" Leif blurted, and then saw the rest of it. It was in her eyes. It was in the way, Smiley said, "It'll be swell working for you, boss." And in the way Turner gave Mr.

Culp the eye, and the Agency back to Big Chris. Then
said to Leif, "Of course you'll buy I.H.C. haying stuff?"

Leif figured a minute, then shook his head at Antie.

"No, he said flatly, "I earn what I get."

Big Chris came over to throw an arm around his slim
shoulders.

"A will is a will, Leif," he said. "A sacred trust. Maybe
you can earn it by raising the swellest colts this country
has ever seen?"

Antoinette caught her breath and looked intently at
Leif.

Suddenly Leif caught what they meant. He laughed
out loud, and started walking toward Big Red.

"Yeah," he said, above the shouts of kids clambering
over Big Red. "The best colts in the world—help build
this country up and how!"

Then down the barn, Rainboy stuck his head over the
top of his stall.

"Yeah," he seemed to snort. "Oh, yeah!"

Everybody laughed.

"Ol' sissy—" the boys yelled. "Ol' Sissy-britches!"

It gave Leif a chance to catch Antie's eye again.

"How about a soda?" he said.

"The best one in the whole world." She nodded,
laughing.

They slipped out the door, and toward a soda stand on
the Fair Midway.

Leif took a deep breath. Boy, did he feel great! Big Chris had his Agency back. That's all he cared—really. Well, almost all. Of course, he still had Big Red. He and Antie.

~~Leslie Mac Donald~~

Leslie Anne MacDonald